A Mischief of Murder

A Jan Christopher Mystery

Helen Hollick

Helen Hollick

Taw River
PRESS

A MISCHIEF OF MURDER

A Jan Christopher Mystery - Episode 6

By Helen Hollick

"As delicious as a Devon Cream Tea!... Miss Read meets The Darling Buds of May in St. Mary Mead!" Elizabeth St.John, author

978-1-0687721-6-0 paperback
978-1-0687721-7-7 e-book

Published by Taw River Press
https://www.tawriverpress.co.uk

READERS' COMMENTS FOR A MIRROR MURDER (EPISODE 1)

"I sank into this gentle cosy mystery story with the same enthusiasm and relish as I approach a hot bubble bath, (in fact this would be a great book to relax in the bath with!) and really enjoyed getting to know the central character, a shy young librarian, and the young police officer who becomes her romantic interest. The nostalgic setting of the 1970s was balm, so clearly evoked, and although there is a murder at the heart of the story, it was an enjoyable comfort read." *Debbie Young, author of the Sophie Sayers cosy mysteries*

"A delightful read about a murder in North-East London. Told from the viewpoint of a young library assistant, the author draws on her own experience to weave an intriguing tale." *Richard Ashen – South Chingford Community Library*

"I spent the entire read trying to decide what was a clue and what wasn't... Kept me thinking. I call that a success."

"I really identified with Jan – the love of stories from an early age, and the careers advice – the same reaction I got – no one thought being a writer was something a working-class girl did! The character descriptions are wonderfully done."

"Brilliant! I'm so enjoying Helen's well-researched murder mystery. I'm not giving anything away here, except to say there's lots of nostalgia, and detail that readers of a certain age (me included) will lap up. A jolly good read. In my opinion, it would make a great television series."

To everyone, past and present, who has, one way or another,
supported a rural
Village Flower and Vegetable Show.

1

AFTERMATH TO MURDER

My fiancé's recovery from severe gunshot wounds had been long, worrying and, for him, extremely frustrating. Those few weeks after Easter 1973 for Laurie and me had passed in a hazed blur of hospitals, police enquiries and a heartbreaking funeral for the other casualty, my murdered library colleague. But that's all part of my previous memoir, and to be honest, I'd rather forget the events of that April.

Laurie's rehabilitation meant we could spend a lot of time together on my days off, the weekends, and of an evening. And once Laurie was partially mobile again we enjoyed a variety of days out courtesy of my Aunt Madge who did the driving – at least until I took my driving test and passed it first time. Which was more luck than judgement, but with a Detective Sergeant as my fiancé and DCI Toby Christopher as my guardian and uncle, I felt obliged not to let the police side down.

Laurie's injuries, broken ribs along with the torn muscles and ligaments to his side and thigh, could have been much worse – even fatal – as bullets do a lot of damage to body and spirit, so by early summer he was becoming more despondent, bored and restless. His parents had come up from where they lived in rural North Devon several times to see him, and on the last occasion, the May Whitsun Bank Holiday, he'd decided to return to the West Country with them.

I didn't mind too much, at least, I put on a brave face, but we were very busy at the library where I worked and I had Aunt Madge's two horses to ride in Epping Forest during what was promising to be the start of a glorious summer, and I had to admit, the cleaner, fresher Devonshire air at the Walker's Valley View Farm would be more beneficial for Laurie than our North London suburban petrol fume fug.

Aunt Madge and I were to holiday in Devon for a week in July, and as it turned out, Uncle Toby was able to join us due to unexpected enforced sick leave. During a rather nasty police incident he'd injured his ankle, tearing several ligaments as a bad sprain, and ended up hobbling on crutches, then a walking stick – and orders from the Commissioner that he was *not* to return to work until he could walk without wincing. Poor Uncle Toby, his disgruntlement hadn't been improved by almost everyone telling him that a sprain was more painful, much worse and much harder to heal, than a fracture. Fractures, he was told, were immobilized by a plaster cast. Sprains were merely bandaged and endured. Although, I have to say, much of the 'endurance' was endured by Aunt Madge and me, having to put up with his exasperating huffy moods. My uncle wasn't usually moody or grumpy (apart from when a particularly nasty or difficult case was proving hard to solve), but I think he was finding that sitting about was becoming exceptionally boring.

Naturally I kept him supplied with books to read, and I did coerce him into reading through the manuscript of the novel I was attempting to write. I'd finished it (it felt marvellous to type the words 'The End'!) but now came the re-writing and editing. I'd convinced my uncle that I needed a new pair of eyes to spot typos and an honest opinion overall. The read-through kept him busy for a week, and I think his opinion of 'most enjoyable' was an honest one. His few suggestions where there were some plot holes, muddled continuity, or scenes that were at odds with the characters' expected actions were all welcome, though.

So, come July, with eager hearts (and one aching ankle), we set off for Devon and a reunion with my fiancé; the horses had been turned loose for their own holiday in a grassy field, and our cleaning lady was to feed our two cats. We piled, bleary-eyed, into my uncle's white Jaguar and headed south-west as dawn was waking up and turning an otherwise grey sky into pink, fingers of sparkling gold, then a beautiful blue.

Little did we know as, Aunt Madge driving, we wended our way along the A roads in the direction of Wiltshire and Salisbury Plain, that in the days ahead mischief would turn into murder...

2

OLD STONES AND OLD PHOTOS
THURSDAY 26TH JULY 1973

Beyond illustrations and photographs in books, I had no recollection of ever seeing the incredible Neolithic monument of Stonehenge, although as we parked the car and walked across the expanse of grass towards the huge standing stones, Aunt Madge informed me that I had been here before.

She elaborated as she fished her camera from its leather carry case, and inspected the lens settings. "You were only just two years old. We were a merry party, you, your twin sister June, your mother and me." She started snapping photos of the stones as she spoke. "I'd offered to drive down to the wedding. Mind, it was February and bitter cold. Even the underwear your mother had knitted didn't do much for the ice chills whipping up our skirts." She laughed as she took another photograph. "My goodness, but the woolly knickers and vest itched! I recall my skin was red raw by the time we reached our hotel. I dropped the darn things straight into the bin, I can tell you!" She laughed again. "No idea what the chambermaid must have thought when she found them the next morning. It was quite a posh hotel. Just as well no one discovered I had no knickers on for the rest of the trip!"

I giggled at the thought of my very sophisticated and elegant aunt wearing home-knitted, scratchy knickers – and then *not* wearing them!

"Why wool?" I asked when I stopped laughing. "You usually wear silk or cotton."

"We were still recovering from the war years, almost everything was home sewn or knitted back then, and your mum had made them as a thank you for doing the driving. I hadn't liked to upset her by not accepting her well-intentioned gift." She added, "Knitted swimsuits were the worst. As soon as you got in the water the wretched things either shrank or expanded, either version ending up revealing far more than was politely desirable. And wet, they weighed a ton."

Fortunately it was now 1973 and those make-do-and-mend days were gone, or so we all hoped, but with various strikes brewing, and rumours of power cuts and three-day weeks being reported for next winter in various newspapers, we feared that those austere days could well return. But for now it was summer and winter's dismal prospects were a long way off. Besides, Laurie thought that Mr Heath might not last much longer as Prime Minister, and the whole political spectrum could change, although Uncle Toby was sceptical about a government under Mr Wilson again, or the Liberals' Jeremy Thorpe. I quite liked Mr Thorpe, but that was because he represented a Devonshire constituency, and I was rather fond of everything Devon. Especially my Devonian fiancé.

That last 1970 General Election when Labour had been soundly thrashed had been my first chance to vote, the age having been lowered from twenty-one to eighteen in 1969. I'd voted Liberal, not being keen on Mr Wilson's poor handling of the economy, and refusing to vote Tory because of that nasty man, Enoch Powell, who had used his election address to re-enforce his dreadful racist demands against black people and to end immigration. Not that I am especially interested in politics, but Aunt Madge had instilled into me the importance of the Suffragette movement, and all that those women had been through in order to get the female sex the vote. I agreed with her. It was my duty, as a woman, to vote and thereby honour their courage.

"What wedding was that?" I asked, returning to the original subject while narrowly missing stepping into a perfectly round splat of cow dung. Why did they have to graze cows where people would be walking? Slightly anxious I took a quick look around as I'd been chased by some cows once – I hadn't trusted them ever since, despite those big, innocent-looking wide eyes they had. Fortunately, the small black-and-white herd was grazing a long way off.

I think Uncle Toby must have noticed my uneasy glance, for, his head slightly tilted back as he inspected the height of the nearest stone, he said, reassuringly, "I expect they have cows or sheep here to save cutting the grass."

"What wedding?" Aunt Madge answered my question. "Your Aunt Susan. Your mother's younger sister married an American army lieutenant. They'd met during his Conscription Service over here, and fell in love."

"And *had* to marry," Uncle Toby added in a low, slightly critical, voice from behind us. He was walking slowly, leaning on his walking stick and trying to pretend he wasn't in pain. Aunt Madge had advised him to stay in the car, but wanting to see the Henge close up he'd ignored her. "She was several months gone, if I recall."

I was slightly taken aback; apart from not knowing that I *had* an Aunt Susan, Uncle Toby was not usually the prudish sort, so I was surprised at his apparent tone of disapproval.

Aunt Madge wasn't prudish either, so her reply did not sound quite so condemning, but nor was it approving. "I know we didn't think much of him, Toby, but Susan was smitten, and nothing anyone said would have changed her mind. She fell pregnant because she wasn't sensible or careful, and was then starting to show. That's why they had to marry in the bitter cold of February. Your mother, Jan, was furious with her, though I never discovered whether it was because she couldn't stand the man in question, the inclement weather, the long journey, or her sister's condition."

"Probably all four," Uncle Toby remarked cynically. "Or you grizzling for the whole journey, Jan." He winked and laughed.

"It was June, who cried a lot," I protested, although I had no idea if that was true.

As twins we were named for the two significant months connected with our birth – conception and premature labour – which is why my full name is January. I never use it unless I have to. "But I don't remember an Aunt Susan?" I queried, frowning, racking my brain to recall her.

"She emigrated with their young children to join Eric after he'd eventually gone back to California in...?" Aunt Madge snapped three more photographs. "Oh, I can't remember when, now."

"Southampton. 1959," Uncle Toby said decisively. "March 1959. I remember it because the next day I was on duty in Trafalgar Square doing my best to hold back

7

an estimated 20,000 demonstrators at a Campaign for Nuclear Disarmament rally. For most of that day I was wishing I'd stowed away with Susan and the kids on the *Queen Mary* rather than receiving bumps and bruises in places I'd rather not mention from those CND people. The women especially; they all seemed to possess sharp elbows."

"Oh yes," Aunt Madge giggled. "I rubbed horse liniment into where you had your worst aches and pains. You stank of it for an entire week!"

I linked my arm through Uncle's, giving him some surreptitious support for his painful ankle. "I do remember the liner. She was enormous!" I exclaimed, surprised at the sudden recollection. "Hundreds of people with streamers and balloons. I must have been…" I paused, working it out, maths was not a strong point of mine. "Six? I have no memory of an aunt though." Nor would Mum or my twin sister have been with us, because by the time I was six they were both dead, as well as my dad. Aunt Madge and Uncle Toby had officially adopted me when I was orphaned at five.

Aunt Madge chuckled. "You cried because a balloon you were holding popped, and the ship's departing horn frightened you."

"It was rather loud," Uncle Toby defended my childhood self. "Nowhere near as loud as that lot in Trafalgar Square though!"

By now we were right beside the stones. From a distance – the carpark – they had looked disappointing, nowhere near as impressive as I'd assumed, but close up was a different matter.

They varied in size. The most prominent Sarsen Stones, forming the outer circle and distinctive horseshoe shape, were about thirteen feet high, while the giant trilithons – a pair of upright lintelled stones –

were even bigger; their uprights (according to the guide book I'd borrowed from the library), reached up to just under thirty-feet and thirty-two feet. The book also said these stones weighed over forty-five tons, though there was nothing to say *how* that fact had been established. The smaller, more varied bluestones, were only about nine feet high, which was quite tiny compared to the other giants.

It was a hot day, and the sun had warmed the stone surfaces. I put my hand onto one, not sure whether to expect it to be stone-cold or baked hot. It was neither. As Goldilocks would say, it was 'just right'. What I did feel was an enormous sense of awe. This monument had stood here for thousands of years, and despite our modern knowledge we had no idea of how they were erected, or what the purpose of the stone circle was for. Ritual, obviously, to do with the midsummer sunrise, but was there more? To commemorate birth, death, the crowning of a king, a special marriage bond? Who knew? The mystery would probably never be solved unless Dr Who, or a similar time-traveller, became a reality.

"There's a good story I read about in one of the newspapers," Uncle Toby said, easing himself down to sit on one of the recumbent stones. "It was rather weird, and might appeal to your liking for fantasy tales, Jan."

I didn't *quite* take offence; I enjoy fantasy novels, but science fiction has been my main passion since I was about twelve. I did wonder if my uncle knew the difference between the two genres, though. My hero was a space smuggler called Radger (rhyme it with 'badger') Knight. A sort of Robin Hood character, with the galaxies being his home instead of Sherwood Forest. I was now re-reading it and taking on board Uncle's suggestions. But if he thought this was fantasy, not science fiction, was I wasting my time? There is a distinct difference between the two, after all. I decided to not worry. My next goal was more important; having corrected all the errors, I intended to find an interested agent or publisher. I was under no illusion, however. It would *probably* not happen. But it *definitely* wouldn't if I didn't try looking.

"So what's this weird story?" I asked. I loved Uncle Toby dearly, but his idea of 'weird' wasn't always the same as mine.

Uncle smiled with indulgent amusement at Aunt Madge who had decided to lie on the ground to get a different photographic perspective of the massive stones.

"Well," he said, "a few years ago, a group of hippies decided to spend the night here in the centre of the circle. They put up a couple of tents, lit a small camp fire – smoked some cannabis – and discussed the nature of the world and the meaning of life, as hippies do. Soon after midnight a wild storm rolled in. Torrential rain, thunder, lightning, the lot. Two of the group got scared and ran to their battered old car. Looking over their shoulders, they saw that the stones were glowing bright blue, so bright they had to look away. They made it to the car and took refuge, then heard screams coming from one of the tents, but the rain was beating down so hard they couldn't open the car doors, all they could do was huddle together in fear. They fell asleep; were woken by the strong sunlight of a beautiful new day. They got out of the car and went towards the stones. Debris was strewn everywhere and all they found were the smouldering remains of the two tents. Of their friends, not a trace. No bodies, no human remains. There was nothing ever seen of the pair again." He stopped talking, his face as straight as a Poker player's with a secretive Royal Flush in his hand.

How awful! My mouth had gone dry, and I felt wobbly. "Is all that true?" I croaked.

"Maybe they're all on that smuggler's spaceship of yours, Jan? The gallant Mr Knight has opted for galactic kidnapping." Aunt Madge suggested.

I frowned. I couldn't imagine my protagonist hero tolerating a group of high-as-kites hippies aboard his beautiful ship, *Excalibur*. (That was also the book's title, by the way: *Excalibur: Flight To The Stars*.) Radger had enough trouble with Electra, his teething baby daughter, and his arch-enemy, Anton Vassal, who looked, in my mind, just like the actor Anthony Valentine who appeared in the British TV spy drama, *Callan*. I had a bit of a crush on him which is probably why I had the (admittedly 'wannabe') writer's visual connection. I quite liked the star actor as well, Edward Woodward, but my liking didn't extend to a secret crush.

Oddly enough, I had no physical 'lookalike' for my Radger character. I knew in my *mind* what he looked like (tall, dark and handsome, naturally), but had no corresponding real-life image. I would instantly recognise him in a crowd, but couldn't describe him beyond that clichéd romantic description. Which worried me because, surely, as a (hopeful) writer I ought to have *some* sort of creative ability to construct a detailed description?

Uncle Toby nudged me from my musing, relented and laughed. "It's amazing how many supposed sensible people – including the National Press – believed that story then, and still do!"

I playfully smacked his arm. Sometimes, his teasing was despicable!

"These great Sarsen stones," he said, peering up to

the top lintel of the nearest megalith, "have been here for thousands of years, built by the power of manual labour and crude stone-age tools. An incredible achievement."

"And when you take into consideration all the outer ditches, the stones at nearby Avebury and the numerous burial mounds," I added, "the whole thing becomes utterly awesome."

"I saw some old photographs at an exhibition some years ago," Aunt Madge said, getting up from her prone position and wiping grass from her skirt, "with Victorian ladies resplendent in their large feathery hats, seated in a pony-drawn trap right beside the stones here. The Victorians were as enthusiastic about inspecting ancient monuments as are we."

"Excuse me?" A male voice interrupted. "I couldn't help overhearing. Are you interested in photography? I have an old photo here that you might like to see."

He was a good-looking young man, about my age (twenty), I guessed, maybe a couple of years younger, with a slight American accent. I heard a very good anecdote once about American and English: A man overheard two women talking in an Arizona bar. He angrily berated them for conversing in 'Mexican'.

"You're in America now, where we talk *English*. So speak English or go back to Mexico."

One of the women looked him up and down, then said, "Well, buddy, we don't talk 'Mexican' around here. We were talking in Native Navajo. If you want to talk English, go back to England."

Very poignant, I thought. Well said, ladies.

Anyway, the young man approached nearer, fishing into his inside jacket pocket and brought out an old and somewhat dog-eared sepia photograph of a man in American Army uniform. He proudly showed it to us.

"That's my Pops leaning against one of these giants. Taken while he was stationed here during the war."

"There were a lot of army chaps here on Salisbury Plain back then," Uncle Toby said, inspecting the photo then handing it to me and Madge. "Still are, come to that."

The man's face in the photo was in partial shadow, so wasn't easily identifiable, his uniform looked crisp and clean, and he was obviously quite a young man, still a teenager.

"We were very grateful to the Americans during the war; you must be proud of him." Aunt Madge said, handing the photo back.

I knew that to be only partially true, for both my aunt and uncle had told me that the USA had only joined in because of the Japanese raid on Pearl Harbour. If that hadn't happened it was still believed that the US President of the time would have remained uninterested in what was happening in Europe. A lot of older Brits still resented the Americans for that, even after the combined victory of the Normandy landings and V.E. Day.

The young man nodded. "I was. He was a good man. He stayed over here after the war, married, had kids – my sister and me – but eventually decided to take us all to the States to live. He passed away, a heart attack, in 1962."

We murmured condolences. It wasn't easy knowing what to say when someone you didn't know mentioned the death of someone else you didn't know.

Aunt Madge neatly changed tack. "Where in America are you from?"

The young man grinned. "Virginia, but Mom remarried an Englishman soon after Pops died and we moved back to England a short while later when I was nine. Mom passed away a few years ago." (More murmured condolences from us.) "I'm here with my stepdad and younger sister touring the West Country before I start Medical College at Cambridge University in the Fall. Although I'm more keen on these old historic sights than Sis is. She's sixteen and only interested in movie stars, fashion and hairdos."

"As most teenagers are," Aunt Madge said, smiling at me because I was the rare exception, although I no longer counted as a teenager. I didn't really care for movie stars, and had long since given up with attempting glamorous hairstyles for my mouse-brown straight hair. My customary ponytail was quite sufficient for most occasions.

"I say," the young man said, "could I ask you to take a photograph of me more-or-less in the same position as Pops? That would be so fab!" He swung a canvas Kodak case from his shoulder and fished out his camera. He went to hand it to Uncle Toby, but Madge stepped in.

"I'm the better photographer," she said. "My husband is either likely to take something with you headless, or with his thumb over the lens."

Uncle Toby guffawed; he had no grounds to deny it. He was a brilliant Detective Chief Inspector, but a hopeless photographer. Fortunately, Chingford Police had their own official cameramen for any serious police work.

Aunt Madge took three photos as requested, and then, joking that he was not to abscond with it, handed him her expensive camera. Obligingly, he took two of us three standing together beside the largest monolith.

Grateful, the young man enthused his thanks, then explained that he ought to get back to his sister waiting in the car. "I'm driving on to meet our stepfather in Bristol, then we're off to Devon and Cornwall. Pa has various business meetings arranged, so while he's working, Sis and I can enjoy ourselves."

"We're off to Devon as well," I said, shaking his proffered hand. "Perhaps we'll bump into each other again?"

It was only later, as we got back into the Jaguar that we realised we'd not asked the young man his name. Not that it mattered, we were unlikely to meet up again.

3

INTERLUDE: LAURIE

I loved Mum and Dad, of course I did, and it was so good of them to put up with my crosspatch frustrated grumbling those past weeks. Don't get me wrong, I loved it there in Devon: the peace and quiet, the clean air, friendly farmers – wild, beautiful views. But I also loved my job. Being a policeman – a good policeman – is all I'd ever wanted to do as a career, right from when I was little. I didn't quite remember it, but Mum said I'd had a toy police pedal car when I was about three, complete with a policeman's helmet and whistle, although I gather that the whistle had very quickly been 'accidentally' lost. I mean, what parent in their right mind gives a three-year-old a whistle?

That helmet was the mainstay of many an old family story because it was far too big for me, so was always slipping down over my forehead to rest on my nose, which, in turn, meant I couldn't see where I was going so was always falling over. I remember the howls when I needed stitches in my chin (I still have a faint scar), from one such tumble. The flooding tears weren't for the gush of blood or the scary, painful, hospital visit, but because I didn't have the beloved helmet with me to hold during the entire distressing ordeal. I clearly remember being upset some years later when I realised the child-sized helmet no longer fitted onto my growing boy's head. I'd long past abandoned the pedal car by then. Funny really, because once I'd joined the Force, I preferred non-uniform C.I.D, which meant no policeman's helmet.

I think, what was worrying me about being 'at home' was that I was enjoying country life again; I feared that when I was fit enough to return to work, I'd not want to go back to North London. Chingford was a nice place – right on the border of the Essex Countryside and the 6,000 or so acres of Epping Forest – but Essex and the London suburban sprawl wasn't the same as rural Devon.

And a lot of my grumpiness was caused by the constant ache in my thigh and left-hand side. Painkillers didn't do much to help. I'd been shot, twice, in April at Easter time, and from what I'd later gathered, it was only thanks to the immediate first aid action by my fiancée's Aunt Madge that I hadn't bled to death there and then. One bullet had smashed through my ribs, the other had gone clean through my thigh. Fortunately, both had missed vital organs and arteries but believe me, bullets are not suitable companions to skin, muscles, ligaments and tendons. At least I was alive. Jan's library colleague hadn't been so lucky. The gunman was now safely banged up for murder and attempted murder, but that wasn't much consolation. If his aim had been better, he might have killed my Jan. I tried not to dwell on that fact too much.

Here we were, near the end of July, and I was still in discomfort and still needed to use a walking stick to get about. It was, actually, a lovely antique Partridge Wood stick with a tine from a Red Deer's antlers as a slightly curved handle and a silver collar hallmarked *Henry*

Howell & Co, London 1835. It had another special, secret, feature as well, but Dad had advised me to keep quiet about it, for, let's say, 'legal' reasons – especially as I *was* a policeman. The stick had belonged to my paternal grandfather and his father before him, so was a family heirloom. The Partridge Wood had originally come from West Africa, and, as my Great Grandad had been a ship's captain, we wondered if he'd acquired the wood for the cane whilst on his seafaring travels. No way of finding out, of course, unless Jan's beloved Dr Who materialised to take me back in time with his T.A.R.D.I.S. Even so, *having* to use it was a bit of a bind, especially when I dropped the thing and had to pick it up. Bending was not a very comfortable movement to do. It is amazing how many things you drop when bending is bloomin' painful! I *was* healing, just too slowly for my liking.

It didn't help that our wonderful old Devonshire farmhouse was half-way down (up?) a long, winding, steep lane. I'm sure the lane wasn't as steep when I used to live there before moving to London! Walking, where hills were concerned, with a stick and a pain in your thigh and side is not to be laughed at. Especially coming *down* hill. Every single muscle protests in the loudest possible way. I do not recommend it. Nor do I recommend being shot by some no-good slug who had held resentment for years. But that's another story and one, as I've already said, I try not to dwell on. Walking sticks do have one advantage. They are superb for relieving pent-up frustrations on overgrown nettles and brambles. A good few hearty thwacks does wonders for a flagging self-morale.

Slugs were not at all popular with my family. Those connected to the no-good criminal kind *and* the other sort. I'm talking the slimy garden variety. You know, homeless snails. (As I thought of them when I was a kid.) Slugs were never popular at any time of the year for a keen gardener like Dad, but come mid-to-late July they were especially abhorred because the last Saturday of the month was the *very* important Village Flower and Vegetable Show. A big, by village standards, event, where anyone who was anyone in many a rural setting vied to become the proud owner of a silver trophy. My village of Chappletawton was no exception to this annual, national, traditional rivalry for a coveted First Place red rosette.

This sort of show had been going since the Victorian age, when they'd been introduced to encourage good practice in horticulture – and to keep the general hoi polloi's gardens tidy. Even small flower shows like ours were judged according to the precise (and to my mind, nit-picky) rules laid down by the Royal Horticultural Society. Rules that had been known to elicit various strategies of cheating, and on occasion in the past, even outright sabotage. Not for the gain of prize money, as the winnings were little more than a recuperation of the few pence per class entrance fee. No, winning was for the prestige of a year-long ownership of a silver trophy and the accompanying gardening expertise kudos.

Dad had won first prize for his dahlias and sweet peas for the last two years in a row. He was aiming for a third, and had similar hopes for his roses, onions, peas and cucumbers. Mum had her eyes on a trophy for the best four hens' eggs, the best hanging basket display, and in cookery, the Victoria Sponge and Scones sections.

"A pity," I said to Dad as we inspected his vegetable patch, "that there's not a 'most slug-or-snail-eaten cabbage' category in the schedule. You'd win that hands down this year."

For some reason, Dad didn't laugh, he only tossed

me a withering look and 'hrrmphed' an unamused grunt.

I gazed around this, the 'business end' part of the garden – Dad's vegetable plot area – to see if there was something more cheering to say. I nodded back down the path towards the white-limed walls of the house. "At least the hanging baskets look good. Very pretty."

Dad grunted again. "They're your mother's entries."

I knew that. It was Mum who had planted the seeds, grown the young plants and transferred them into the willow basket holders, then diligently tended the result (in various weathers), deadheading the plethora of trailing lobelia, geranium and colourful petunias and begonias every day. I'd mentioned them to Jan during a telephone call and she'd giggled, telling me that to most people making hanging basket holders was a new craze, with dozens of the things being fashioned as macramé with no practical use whatsoever, apart from decorative plant pot holders.

Mum also complained about slugs and snails. Why these slithery creatures bothered to heave their way up the side of the rough cob walls to nibble on pretty flowers when, at Dad's end of the garden, there were more enticing cabbages and such to dine on, was beyond me. Maybe the answer was because Dad had declared war and used any trick he could think of to annihilate the trespassers, while Mum solemnly collected them in a bucket and tossed them over the hedge into the lane. (Mum firmly resisting the suggestion that any that didn't get squashed by passing tractors or cars, only slithered back into the garden again after dark.)

"The tomatoes look nice and fat," I offered tentatively. "Shouldn't they be red, though, not green?" Dad pulled a face. Oops. I'd blundered. I moved to a different patch, pointed at something I knew should be green. "The peas look good."

Dad sniffed loudly and, picking a single pea pod from its stick-twining vine-like tendril, snapped it open to reveal a row of round, green peas within. He selected one, popped it into his mouth, pulling various faces as he munched, much as a wine-taster would sample a fine Burgundy. He selected another and handed it to me. I took it, ate it, making the same expressions. I had no idea what I was supposed to be tasting or what to say.

I opted for: "Hmm, crunchy. Nice and sweet."

The right thing, as Dad smiled. "You can't be too careful with peas. Regular watering during cropping deters mildew, but I take care not to wet the leaves. I water at the base of my plants, not over them. Can't risk sunburnt leaves."

I immediately envisioned cartoon peas wearing sunglasses and stretched out on sun loungers beside a sparkling swimming pool, relaxing and catching a few rays.

Dad didn't notice my inattention, for he was rambling on about good pea care. "The compost can dry out in hot weather, too, so regular watering is essential. Did I tell you someone pilfered a few sackfuls from my compost heap back when you got shot? During those days when we were up visiting you? As if people can't make their own compost! Though, I grant, there's more to it than just chucking garden waste into a heap... anyway, as I was saying, mice are a problem with peas, and your mother's bloomin' hens if they get out from their run. Nigh on gobbled my entire crop a few years back."

I was at college in Exeter then, and remembered the hens incident very well. World War Three had almost broken out between Mum and Dad, and I'd worried about possibly having to eat Revenge Chicken for weeks afterwards.

Dad leant forward and extracted a snail from the pea tendrils. It had a pretty coloured shell which it immediately retreated into. I winced as Dad dropped the snail onto the gravel path and deliberately stepped on it, the breaking shell an audible *crunch*. Was I being ridiculous feeling sorry for a tiny snail? He – she? Snails are simultaneous hermaphrodites, which means they have both male and female reproductive organs in order to compensate for a bad breeding season. (It's amazing what useless information I can recall from school science lessons!)

"What are these?" I asked, pointing towards one of several empty tins scattered here and there among various vegetable and flower foliage. I peered closer at the nearest, discovered that it wasn't empty. I wrinkled my nose at the disgusting sludge within.

"Beer traps," Dad said. "Put beer in the bottom and the slugs and snails love it. They get drunk and drown."

"Like the brother of Richard III. He drowned in beer, didn't he?"

Dad shook his head. "Thrust headfirst into a butt of Malmsey Wine. That's how he was executed for treason. In the 1400s I think it was."

I shrugged. "Not a bad way to go, is it? Drowning in beer or wine."

"Better than shrivelling up after being doused in salt – which I don't do out here in the garden. Salt would contaminate the soil and be as disastrous for my plants. Salt is for fish and chips and salt and vinegar crisps, not my soil."

I could quite see why Mum preferred to simply toss her captured molluscs over the hedge.

I tilted my head to one side. Was that a car? I

listened intently. The sound of an approaching vehicle always echoed and rumbled down the lane... Yes, definitely a car! We were not expecting any deliveries, and the postman had long since come and gone, so I hoped it would be...

As quickly as I could hobble, I went to the garden gate that led into the lane, just in time to see a white Jaguar carefully negotiate the tight bend where an oak tree leaned a little far over, and ease past the over-exuberant growth of bracken, bramble, nettle and more pleasing campion, vetch, dandelion, valerian, rosebay willowherb, foxglove and honeysuckle... the wild flowers I knew. There were more that I didn't know.

I grinned, waved my stick in greeting as the car drew to a sedate halt. They were here at last, my boss, DCI Toby Christopher, his wife, Madge and my dearest loveliest, fiancée, Jan! My grin widened as she threw the rear passenger door open and jumped out to fling her arms around me. Any stranger watching would have thought we'd been apart for months, not a mere few weeks.

I couldn't help noticing that on the back seat was her faithful old teddy bear, Bee Bear. OK, I was a tad jealous; that bear went everywhere with her! And probably got more cuddles than I did.

Madge was driving, she too got out of the car and gave me a hug. I'm pleased to say, my boss simply shook my hand.

"Mum's had the kettle simmering atop the Aga this past half-hour," I said. "Park the car in the usual place down by the barn, then come in and have a cup of tea. I expect you're gasping. I won't guarantee cake, as all the baking this week has been geared for the village show."

"Actually," Jan said, doing a little hop and skip jump, "I want the loo. Somewhat desperately!"

4

CREAM TEA

Indoors, I was 'relieved' and feeling far more comfortable. The whole house was filled with the delicious aroma of baking. And despite Laurie's doubts, there was cake along with the tea… well, scones, freshly made that afternoon with a lashing of thick cream and fruit-filled homemade strawberry jam. Cream first on scones, by the way; jam first is the Cornish tradition, and there's quite a bit of rivalry between the two opposing theories. Mostly friendly banter. But not always. You can easily remember what way it should be: when making a sandwich you spread the butter (dairy) first, then the jam. So it's the same for scones. Cream (butter) first, then the jam. But it's up to you whether you say scone as in 'gone' or scone as in 'stone'. Both, believe it or not, are correct. And here's a joke for you: How did the scone react to the butter's exaggerated compliment? 'You're buttering me up!' Ha ha.

We sat at the old kitchen table, which a small army could have fitted round if squashed up a little. It was certainly big enough to have accommodated a Queen Victoria-sized family – the era it had been lovingly made in. Maybe it was my writer's imagination, but I could clearly see, in my mind, such figures from the past sitting alongside us. Mater, Pater and a horde of smartly dressed children, their hair brushed, their faces shiny clean. The Walkers' Devonshire farmhouse was filled with echoes of the past that lingered from the sturdy foundations right up to the oak roof beams. The house had been built in the late eighteenth century and it was not hard to envision the families who had previously lived here. I was certain their spirits remained, not to haunt, but to keep a genial eye on the place. Elsie, Laurie's mum, had told me on my previous visits that she didn't think of the old farmhouse as hers. "Mr Walker – Alf – and I, are simply the present custodians." I liked that idea. With the way the wooden floorboards creaked, the slates on the kitchen floor were worn and the pervading atmosphere of love and laughter filled each room, it was easy to agree with her sentiment.

"Are these the scones you're entering for the village show, Mum?" Laurie asked through a mouthful of cream and jam, crumbs sticking to his lips and the faint fuzz of whiskers where he hadn't shaved as carefully as he would have done for work. "They certainly taste like winning entries."

"Oh no," Elsie replied, plonking a hefty dollop of jam atop a pile of cream, "these are just practices. I'll make my show entries tomorrow."

"Well, if these are practices," Uncle Toby laughed, "I can't wait to taste the final versions. I assume we'll eventually get a chance to eat the show entries?"

"Oh, no fear of that," Alf laughed. "We'll be eating scones, Victoria Sponge and homemade jam for the rest of the year!"

Elsie batted him lightly round the head with a tea towel. "And we'll be eating your veg for even longer!"

"Ah," Alf chuckled, "but my onions, cucumbers and peas are prize-winning varieties, so worth eating. After they've been judged and won a prize, that is!"

"Along with the Olympic-grade snails?" Laurie added. We all laughed.

"Are you still happy to judge our crafts section, Madge?" Elsie asked, a little apprehensively. "The committee agreed with Heather, our shopkeeper's suggestion, that asking you was an inspired idea, but none of us wanted to pressure you into anything."

"Oh no, it's an honour to be asked and I'll be delighted to do it!" Aunt Madge answered. "I've been reading up on what and what not to look for. I'm actually quite excited about the prospect."

"You'll change your mind after," Alf corrected. "Prepare yourself for comments like, 'The judge wouldn't know a darning needle from a knitting needle'."

"Or, 'The judge can't tell the difference between a running stitch and a stem stitch'."

"Or, 'Plain from purl'."

We giggled together as we thought up more silly derogatory comments – none of which applied to my aunt who was a superb seamstress, unlike myself. I couldn't even thread a needle without getting frustrated, and when I did try sewing, the thread always – without fail – got tangled and knotted.

"Who else will be judging?" Aunt Madge asked when we'd finished laughing.

Elsie answered. "Beatrice Norbutt will be judging cookery and preserves. You might know her better as Beatrice Pye the TV cook? She's a stalwart of the village and always judges because, naturally, she'd rather not enter anything."

"We met her the other Christmas when we were here," I said. "A lovely lady. Very homely." That was the Christmas when I'd first met Alf and Elsie Walker, and when Laurie had proposed on New Year's Eve. And, I'm ashamed to say, when I'd been somewhat jealous (wrongly) about a previous girlfriend.

"Indeed she is a very nice woman," Elsie agreed, "and she is fair with her judging, especially in the children's sections. She tries to ensure they all get a prize one way or another, or if not, she tries to give some sort of encouraging praise, but doesn't always manage it."

Alf guffawed. "Aye, last year young Mary-Anne Culpin entered the 'Most Cabbage White Butterflies collected in a jar'…"

Horrified, I interrupted; "Oh, the poor things, how can they breathe all squashed in together, and how on earth do they get counted?"

"They're dead, silly," Laurie said, laughing but squeezing my hand at the same time. "Gardeners hate them because they eat everything, so such a competition is well approved of."

I queried this as it didn't sound right. "But butterflies don't eat plants. They look for nectar in the flowers."

"Quite right," Alf replied, "but they do lay dozens of eggs on brassicas, things like cabbages for instance, hence their name, and the eggs hatch into caterpillars which munch their way through an entire crop leaving only a bare skeleton of the plant."

"So why," I questioned, "isn't the competition a 'how many Cabbage White Caterpillars in a jar'?"

Alf chuckled. "Good point, but I think the idea is to help rid us of the butterflies. But in this case, it was realised that Mary-Anne had kept her collection from the previous year and simply added more to it. Miss Norbutt – while in confidence was amused at the ingenuity – gave the girl a sound ticking off for mischievous cheating."

"And," Elsie said with a firm nod of her head, "we immediately introduced the rule that the contents of any such collection were discarded by a committee member after being counted and recorded. So no chance of such mischief again."

I could see the gardeners' point of view, but still suppressed a shudder. Nuisance Cabbage Whites or not, I didn't like the thought of deliberately killing them for the sake of a competition. There again, I suppose the slugs and snails were just as callously slaughtered for the same reason. The only difference, butterflies were much prettier. Even the white ones.

I decided to stop thinking about it and changed to a different topic. "Mary-Anne Culpin? Wasn't she the little minx last summer who kept moving that old scarecrow around and playing tricks on the villagers?"

"That's her," Elsie confirmed. "She's not a bad girl, just always up to mischief of one sort or another."

I'd rather liked her. I think she played tricks because she was bored and wanted attention. That's the downside of village life; outside of school or helping their parents there wasn't much for children to do.

We went quiet for a moment, collectively remembering the other events of that summer of sunshine and haymaking, when murder had, again, come to the village.

Uncle Toby asked, "Was Dotty Dorothy's husband ever found?"

Poor Dorothy Clack, she was murdered as well, but had a reputation of often being off with the fairies, or in that instance, a leprechaun. Her husband was a salesman or something – I couldn't remember the detail, all I recalled was that he was rarely at home.

Alf poured himself another cup of tea, offered

another to all of us. Aunt Madge accepted, I declined. He explained, "Oh, he was found only a short while ago, living a completely different life with a different woman. Apparently poor Dorothy had driven him round the bend with her fancies, so he just upped and left, sending her a small monthly allowance to stop her looking for him. It seems she was probably none the wiser about his alternative life. He's not been welcome in the village, needless to say. Dorothy Clack was an eccentric soul, but she was well liked. From what we gather, he was something to do with a profitable car sales business up North. Now that all the legal matters are finally cleared up and probate has gone through, the cottage is up for sale and we'll all be pleased when it's sold and he clears off for good. Takers are wary, though, of buying somewhere where someone has been murdered. Too scared of ghosts, I guess."

"If ever there was a ghost hanging around it would be Dotty Dorothy!" Elsie laughed. "She was as mad as a hatter, but underneath all her nonsense, she had a heart of gold."

"I'd be quite happy to buy a place in a lovely country village – with or without a ghost – if it was just what I wanted," Madge announced. Both I and Uncle Toby looked sharply at her. Where did that come from, and what did she mean by it?

"And who is judging the flowers and vegetables?" Uncle Toby asked, a little ruffled, I thought, but obviously intending to set the mood back to something more convivial, and to steer away from the alarming subject of moving house.

"Rose Carpenter. The star gardener from TV's *In Rose's Garden*. Her place is a couple of miles outside the village," Elsie said, but didn't sound as enthusiastic as she had when talking about Beatrice Norbutt.

"That's the programme where she visits gardens round the country isn't it?" Aunt Madge asked.

Elsie nodded.

My aunt frowned. "I confess, I rarely watch it, she always seems a bit..." she paused, went on, "... supercilious?"

"Haughty, arrogant, rude and opinionated would be more accurate," Elsie snorted. "But we have to put up with her as a judge as she expects the prestige, and if she didn't judge she'd enter every class and expect to win hands down. Getting her to judge is the lesser of two evils."

"Or the lesser of two snails?" Uncle Toby joked.

I did know of Rose Carpenter, having seen her face in several magazines and on the cover of two books – I'd never watched the TV show, not being especially interested in gardening. To me she always looked over-made-up with stylish, expensive clothes, coiffured hair and bright red-painted nails. Not the sort of person you'd associate with hands-on gardening.

I somehow couldn't imagine her catching Cabbage White butterflies to put in a jam jar for a competition. She'd be the sort to spray everything – and kill everything – with DDT or something similar.

5

A RUMOUR OF MISCHIEF

Because Elsie had been slaving over a hot stove all day (well, a hot Aga), and despite stuffing ourselves with scones, we agreed to go up to the village pub for dinner that evening. I didn't need my arm twisting, having previously experienced the wonderful meals at Chappletawton's Exeter Inn public house. There was no resistance to the idea from any of us Townie Londoners.

The pub always had a friendly atmosphere, enhanced by an open welcome for well-behaved dogs, affirmed by their own resident canine, Frankie. Golden, curly haired Frankie was one of those dogs with a constantly wagging tail at one end and a wide, doggie smile at the other while waiting patiently and expectantly beside the tables for illicitly offered scraps. Despite the 'Please don't feed Frankie' notice on the first page of the menu book. (But then, Frankie couldn't read, so was unaware of the rule.)

After a rather large, but very tasty, portion of Coq au vin I really didn't have the room, but I managed to squeeze in a pudding – a scrummy Eton Mess. (Summer fruits with meringue and a scoop of clotted cream.) I know; I ought to have been watching my weight, but had given up on that futile lark months ago! We were relaxing with an after dinner Irish coffee when Heather, a friend of the Walkers, came into the pub, saw us, and with a broad smile came over to say hello. Naturally, she was invited to join us. Despite the smile she looked rather frazzled. Alf ordered her a large G & T.

I'd met Heather several times before as she was the owner and postmistress of the village shop, combined with being the local news-spreader, although much of it was gossip rather than news. Typical for a village like Chappletawton, word could spread faster than a swooping kestrel. Heather had her finger on the pulse of village life, however, and if anything needed to be done it was always best to ask her because she would bend over backwards to ensure it got done. That old saying: 'If you want something done – ask a busy person.'

Heather, in addition to all her other roles, was the secretary for the Village Show, one reason for the frazzled look. I'd been secretary for our stableyard fun riding club for three years, and even with only a modest twenty members it often proved hard work. Organising things is *never* as easy as it first appears. Usually because there is always someone who doesn't want something done the way it was being done. This sort of person never wanted to take on the responsibility of running things though.

Heather plonked herself down in a chair, puffed her cheeks and took a large, grateful, gulp of her gin. "You'd not believe the number of people who have asked me if they can put in a late entry. I mean, no they can't, entries closed yesterday, and closed *means* closed. I've already written out all the entry labels and I'm not going to write out any more."

We made a few sympathetic noises while she carried on chattering nineteen to the dozen. "Beatrice Norbutt is our second judge – oh, you are still happy to be our craft judge aren't you Madge? Please say you are, finding someone else at this late stage would be a nightmare."

"My wife will make a very good crafty judge," Uncle Toby joked. "She knows all the tricks of the trade."

Heather looked appalled. "Are you suggesting our competitors cheat? I assure you they don't..." She paused, went slightly pink. "Well, not usually. It was discovered last year that Mrs Pyke had bought her flowering pot plant from the local garden centre. She was remiss enough to have left the price tag on it. Then there was that year when all except one rose grower developed foot rot, or something, overnight just before the show."

"Foot rot is for sheep," Alf corrected. "Don't you mean black spot?"

"No, that's Macbeth," Elsie interjected.

Laurie frowned. "Macbeth is a red spot, I think. Lady Macbeth's bloodied hands 'Out, out damn spot'."

Aunt Madge added her two pennyworth. "P.G. Wodehouse mentions a black spot in his *Joy in the Morning*. I love some of the characters' names he came up with; this one is Boko Fittleworth."

I might have guessed she'd mention something from Wodehouse as she'd read all his books at least twice. She maintained that they cheered her up on wet winter weekends.

I corrected all of their theories. "The Black Spot is from *Treasure Island*. It was given to Long John Silver as a sign that he was to be dumped as Captain, but he pointed out that the round spot was made from paper taken from a Bible, so whoever had made it would be the one cursed for defacing the Lord's Word and that, in consequence, he himself was quite safe."

Heather's expression was that of bewilderment. "Roses get black spot?"

"Yes," Alf pointed out, "but it's a fungal virus that spreads. They couldn't have all suddenly got it overnight."

"And I rather think you meant greenfly, dear," Elsie added with a gentle smile. "We had a bad bout of greenfly a few years back – the entire village was infected, but thankfully, we also had an inundation of ladybirds."

Nodding enthusiastically at having sorted out the muddle, Heather clapped her hands. "Oh yes, I remember, ladybirds were everywhere. Even in my shop. It was that very hot summer, and because of them we all had to keep our windows and doors closed."

"And I think you'll find that was in June, so nothing to do with the show," Alf said.

"Anyway," Elsie shot him a disapproving glance before saying, "Madge here has already told me that she's looking forward to judging alongside Rose Carpenter and Beatrice, so I think we're all sorted."

Heather beamed with pleasure. "I assume you've heard of Rose Carpenter, Mrs Christopher? We've managed to nab her to be our judge again this year. She lives outside the village at Rose Cottage Garden – a wonderful place, about three acres of beautiful gardens and woodland. The bluebells there in spring are just heavenly. Such a pity she rarely opens the place to the public, but of course, you often see it on TV. Especially wonderful now that television is in colour – if you're lucky enough to have a colour TV, that is." She paused to sip her drink. "Of course, we had to really twist her arm to be our judge again, but we were lucky they've finished filming for this year; she thinks there will be a new series in the autumn, although Rose hasn't said much about it, so I assume it's all hush-hush at the moment. Apparently," Heather leant forward slightly and lowered her voice, "apparently, the producer, or director or someone like that, is down here to see her tomorrow, so I expect we'll hear a lot more in the evening at the Squire's Buffet Do … I say, you are invited, aren't you? I can fix it if not…"

Patting her arm, Alf laughed. "Heather, my dear, I am the show treasurer and Elsie is one of the stalwarts of the committee, so of course we're invited – along with Laurie, Jan, Madge and Toby. I've already arranged it."

Elsie explained to us that the 'Squire' always hosted a buffet supper on the evening before the show in order to give a pre-show thank you to all the committee and helpers. I've no idea why he was called that, as he wasn't the village squire, but plain Captain Frank Dowd, although he did live in the Manor at the edge of the village, which used to be the Squire's domain back before World War One, so I expect that accounted for the semi-serious nickname.

"The Squire is hoping to win with his roses again this year, Alf," Heather said, as she smiled with relief – at something else she didn't need to organise, I guessed. Pointing at Alf, she clarified, "These two men take it in turns to win various trophies two years running, but they've never managed to make it a *third*. Three in a row means they are given a special trophy to keep."

"And so far, it hasn't happened," Alf answered confidently. "But 1973 might be my lucky year."

"At least this year we don't have any of poor Dorothy Clack's supernatural nonsense to deal with," Heather said with a sigh. "I mean, bless her, she was a dear soul, but there was more than one in the village who would have openly accused her of witchcraft. Those greenfly and ladybirds didn't come from nowhere, you know, and what about the year we had frost right into May? Or those downpours literally the day before the show which battered everyone's gardens to shreds?"

"What about them?" Aunt Madge asked innocently, though I noticed Elsie surreptitiously trying to signal her to not say anything.

My aunt didn't notice, nor did Heather, who launched into her next tale.

"Well, there was more than one who'd seen Dotty Dorothy out and about in the moonlight on the days before the show. Apparently wandering round the village casting some supposed fairy dust around. I say 'fairy dust', it looked more like silver Christmas glitter. She said it was to encourage the flowers to bloom, though there was more than one in the village who quietly insisted she was a witch casting spells to kill off any rival show entries. Which was daft because Dotty only entered the chutney, jam and homemade wine classes. The chutneys and jams were all right, but the wines would have made suitable drain cleaner they were that potent."

Laurie chuckled. "Maybe she could have marketed it as a snail and slug deterrent?"

Heather agreed. "One sip and we'd have had inebriated molluscs throughout the village. Poor Frank, he said he's having great trouble with snails. And did you hear about Geoff Winters?"

We all looked expectantly at her. What about Geoff Winters? Not that I knew who he was.

Heather leant forward slightly again and glanced over her shoulder to ensure no one else was listening.

"Someone broke into his greenhouse. Pulled up all his tomatoes, then stamped on them. Squashed the lot."

Our combined astonished outrage erupted.

"No!"

"Never!"

"That's terrible!"

"Has he reported it to the police?" Uncle Toby asked, frowning. "That would count as trespass and vandalism."

"It would, I agree," Alf interrupted – he'd been the only one not to make any shocked exclamation – "except Geoffrey Winters doesn't have a greenhouse."

We stared at him.

"The greenhouse in question was Roger Kyte's, the incident was over a month ago, and it was his geese that did the damage because he'd left the door open."

Heather blushed. "Was it really? I only heard about it the other day."

None of us were sure if that was true or if she was simply covering for her error. It didn't matter, it wasn't important.

"You'll be all right there then Dad," Laurie said. "We don't have geese."

"Nor does it matter about my toms, they're nowhere near ready for the show. There isn't a category for green tomatoes," Alf pointed out wistfully.

"Yet," Elsie said with a grin. "I am thinking of getting two geese. A pair. Goose and gander – and perhaps some peacocks?"

"You are *not* getting peacocks," Alf stated. "They roost on the roof and 'meow' all the time."

"That's cats." Elsie contradicted. "The 'meow' bit, not the roof."

"We had a kitten that got onto the roof once." Heather launched into another anecdote. "We'd called her Badger because she was black and white. Woke us up early hours of one morning shrieking away at the top of her voice. My husband and I ran outside, he in his 'jamas, me in my curlers and nightie, thinking she must have been severely injured or something. Couldn't see her anywhere, but still that awful noise. I looked up, shone my torch onto the roof, and there she was right up on the ridge where you usually see straw foxes, pheasants or hares. We had one heck of a job to coax her down. That was one of her nine lives gone. Soon after she fell into a water butt, only by chance I saw it happen, then she got locked in a cupboard for two days. Next, she was found as a stowaway in the postman's van – just as well that she had a collar and name tag on. She got kicked by a pony and went tumbling along the lane like a bowling ball – then went on to have six litters of kittens and lived until she was at least fifteen."

"Actually," Aunt Madge clarified as soon as she could get a word in edgewise, "we have peacocks at our stableyard, about ten of them, and yes, they do roost on the owner's house and barn roof – and they do make a meow sound, though mostly only in spring when they're pairing up. Otherwise, they honk, similar to geese. I quite like them, they're intelligent birds, you know."

"Geese and roosters are much noisier," I added. We had geese up at the stables as well. The gander – he was called Lenin – had a thing about attacking the hubcaps of cars. Presumably because they were silver and shiny and reflected his image so he assumed it was another invading gander. I'd long since learnt how to deal with him when he rushed you, head lowered, wings flapping, hissing like Nagaina, the infuriated cobra in Kipling's *Rikki-Tikki-Tavi*. The way to deal with them was not to run, stand your ground, raise your arms and hiss back. It usually worked.

"Excellent guard dogs, geese," Uncle Toby offered.

"Guard Geese," Laurie corrected.

"And they'd guard your greenhouse from any secretive mischief-maker," Heather suggested.

"I don't care whether they giggle, gaggle, sit on the roof or put themselves into the oven for Christmas dinner; we are *not* having geese or peacocks," Alf insisted.

He sounded pretty firm and determined. I exchanged a grin with Laurie, who whispered, "Which means Mum will, sooner rather than later, be getting geese and peacocks."

6

TROWEL TROUBLE

FRIDAY 27TH JULY 1973

Friday dawned wet and miserable, a contrast to the sunshine we'd had on the journey down. It was July but as cold as winter on account of an evil wind that seemed to be coming straight from the salt mines of Siberia. Laurie and I took the Walkers' friendly old Labrador, Bess, for a walk up the lane after breakfast – she loved it, but I was reminded of the Aesop fable about the North Wind and the Sun, where they argue about which is stronger, and decide to test their ability by trying to make a traveller remove his coat. The wind blows harder and colder, but the man clasps his coat tighter and tighter, then the sun shines hotter and hotter and the man removes his coat. I think the moral of the tale is meant to be something about gentleness wins over brute force. A lesson a lot of us could learn, maybe?

The rain passed over briefly, skittering across the valley, but fortunately we'd reached home by the first spattering so it didn't really matter. Aunt Madge and Uncle Toby had gone exploring to visit Arlington Court with its National Trust Carriage Museum; a Regency house and impressive collection of different types of horse-drawn vehicles, along with picturesque gardens situated on the edge of Exmoor.

Elsie was cooking in her kitchen, and Alf was ensconced in his greenhouse. Laurie had his mind riveted on the cryptic crossword in a newspaper, so I settled down to continue editing my novel. Alf had very kindly allowed me to make use of his office, as he said I could spread my manuscript out on his desk. (He'd also mentioned that all his accountancy clients' details were locked away – he was a respected accountant, so had highly private financial information.)

I liked Alf Walker's office, even though it was normally his hallowed territory. It was cosy and comfortable with one large window overlooking the garden and the magnificent view over this part of the Taw Valley. His desk was one of those large Victorian mahogany pedestal affairs, with a top inset of dark green leather, and three drawers beneath. To the side of the central kneehole were twin pedestals with three drawers each, fitted with intricate brass handles. A gorgeous piece of furniture, the only fly in the ointment was Alf's very large, very heavy, typewriter which I had to heave out of my way. The office walls were lined with bookshelves, except one bay which embraced filing cabinets tucked behind a wooden façade cupboard, above which were a few shelves of box files. The other shelves were filled from floor to ceiling with fiction – thrillers – and non-fiction travel books, both being Alf's great passion.

Naturally, before I settled to my own 'work' I had a quick browse; there were a lot of spy thrillers, Ian Fleming, John le Carré and such, plus every one of the twenty *Jack Dreamer* novels by A.L. Frederick. I admit I wasn't usually keen on spy thrillers, but I adored that series. Dreamer was an MI6 agent who worked undercover as an international hotel inspector, which conveniently took him to all sorts of different countries and landed him in all sorts of adventures with all sorts of other secret agents – goodies and baddies – and several women, all beautiful, some nice, some nasty. Jack Dreamer was a gentleman, who did his best to get the job done, but he wasn't infallible, which made the books extra interesting. He didn't always succeed in his assignments. By comparison, James Bond, I always thought, was often a little too far-fetched and he was too much of a womaniser. I know everyone raved over Sean Connery, but I wasn't one of the smitten. The Jack Dreamer books were plausible, entertaining and extremely readable. The only negative thing about them, the author was a recluse using a pen name and no one (except his agent one assumed), knew who he was. I was convinced that 'he' was a 'she' and probably a member of the royal family. (My money was on Princess Margaret.) Or maybe the author was a genuine, retired spy who was forbidden from exposing his/her identity because of the Official Secrets Act? I knew all about that because Uncle Toby had worked at a place called Bletchley Park during the war and wasn't allowed to talk about it. All I knew was that he had something to do with maps. And Aunt Madge had worked with Churchill, so there were lots of things she couldn't talk about either. Ideal spy stuff, though!

I settled happily into reading through what was supposed to be the final version of my manuscript, which, I admit, was not on the same level as the Jack Dreamer books, but, I hoped at least showed potential. To my dismay, I found several silly typos (how had I managed 'bread stubbled chin' instead of 'beard stubbled'?). I felt that the plot and action read well, at a good, consistent pace. Or at least, I thought so. I was probably deluding myself, but such are the aspirations of optimistic writers.

I'd managed to read through an entire chapter when the peace and quiet was disturbed by a heavy thumping at the front door, which was ominous, as in the countryside everyone who knew what was what used the *back* door for informal visits. Front doors were for the vicar or strangers, or, as it turned out, Barnstaple Police. I heard Laurie talking to someone – male voices. He popped his head round the office door, asked me to come into the sitting room while he went to fetch his dad from the greenhouse.

I was dismayed to discover that the visitor was none other than Detective Sergeant Frobisher. We'd had run-ins with him before, an arrogant, very rude man who always rubbed Laurie – and me – up the wrong way with his snide, ungentlemanly remarks. Mind, the last time we were here in Devon Aunt Madge had soundly put him in his place – twice. Being on the sharp end of her tongue is not for the faint hearted. And matters had come to a head (well, a bloody nose), when Laurie had firmly punched him for being offensive to me. There was rumour after that about Frobisher seeking a transfer to somewhere in London, with my uncle sounded out about being obliging. Thankfully, nothing came of it. It seemed pretty clear to me that DS Frobisher had the Green Eyed Problem: he was jealous of the better, more capable policeman… my Laurie. I rather hoped that the uneasy truce the pair of them had managed to agree on that last time was still holding.

I didn't offer coffee, merely explained that Mrs Walker was busy in the kitchen and would not appreciate being disturbed, although she did pop her head round the door, asked if all was well and did we want coffee?

Frobisher answered before I could say anything. "No. I need a word with Mr Walker."

He didn't add a please or thank you.

Alf came in from the garden via the patio doors, stood on the mat just inside. "Mucky boots," he explained pointing to his boot-clad feet. "What can I do for you Detective Sergeant?"

"Where were you yesterday evening, Mr Walker?"

"Why do you need to know?" came the immediate, slightly guarded response.

"Just answer the question."

Laurie came up behind his dad, frowned at Frobisher. "Is this an official line of enquiry, or something general?" he snapped with more rudeness than politeness.

"Official. Not that it is any of your business."

Ah, the hatchet hadn't been buried then.

"I do know I have my rights," Alf responded to the bristling hostility fizzing between Laurie and DS Frobisher, "but as I have nothing to hide, young man, I can answer quite openly. From 7.30 I was partaking of a rather pleasant dinner at the Exeter Inn along with my family. In which I include DCI Christopher and his wife."

Frobisher ignored the reference to my uncle and aunt. "And at what time did you leave those premises?"

"Just gone ten. We were not there after closing, if that's what you're driving at."

Frobisher's expression was a cross between annoyance and embarrassment. "You did not go anywhere else? Nipped out for a few minutes or anything?"

"Apart from a brief visit to the Gents', I did not. We came home, talked for a while then went to bed."

"You didn't make a quick visit to the far end of the village while at the pub? Pop along to White Gates, for instance?"

"Jack's place? No, why would I? I'd have had no reason to be calling on him at that time of night. He's elderly and set in his ways. It's well known that he goes to bed by nine. Up with the lark, bed with the owl. Bob Featheridge, his immediate neighbour, might have called in to see he was settled for the night. They're good friends. Share a pleasure in gardening."

"Featheridge? I've already spoken to him. He says he was at work until late. Preparing for this village show fiasco. And you are adamant you didn't leave the house during the night?"

"I assure you, DS Frobisher, our village show is no fiasco, as you put it. But what is this, Sergeant? I'm adamant I did not go anywhere near Jack's. Having enjoyed a hearty meal, a few glasses of wine and a brandy, I went to bed and slept like the proverbial log until about eight this morning when I got up, came downstairs, let the dog out and put the kettle on. The postman came at about 8.30 with a letter to be signed for. I expect he'll vouch I still had my pyjamas on."

"What's all this about?" Laurie demanded, having lost patience at staying silent.

"Jack Donaldson was found dead in his garden early this morning. Mr Featheridge, a locally employed gardener, has stated that he saw Mr Donaldson pottering about at 7 p.m. last night, a time he is certain of because the church ringers started their nuisance bell ringing practice. Nuisance being his words, not mine, although I am inclined to agree with him. The M.O. has reason to assume Donaldson died between then and 10 p.m.," Frobisher announced as dispassionately as if he were talking about the weather. He was plainly disgruntled that Alf had a cast iron alibi. He added in a tone that would have suited a medieval hangman, "There are suspicious circumstances that we need to investigate. Can you explain why a gardening implement, with your initials painted on the handle, was clutched in Donaldson's hand?"

"Jack? Dead?" Alf repeated, incredulously. "Why would anyone want to kill Jack? He is – was – a harmless, gentle old soul."

Frobisher's reply was thick with cynicism. "A serious rival to this Village Show nonsense, perhaps?"

Alf laughed. "That sort of rivalry is taking things a bit far, and, I'm afraid, son, no one would take Jack as a rival anyway."

Frobisher's frown darkened. Alf calling him 'son' was probably not a good idea. "Not a rival, eh? And why would that be?" he snapped.

"Because, Detective Sergeant, Jack took pleasure in his garden, occasionally entered one or two classes for the show, but never expected to win anything because he didn't take that sort of thing seriously. If a cabbage had a caterpillar on it he left it there, if a rose had rust on a leaf, he still entered it. He wasn't a rival to anyone."

"And the tool, sir? Can you explain why he had *your* trowel in his hand?"

"I can if it's an old red-handled one you're talking about. I gave it to him last summer because his had broken and I had one I didn't need. I have several trowels. I tend to be given them as birthday presents."

I made a mental note of that. *No gardening tools as gifts for Alf.*

"Are you certain about foul play?" Laurie asked. "Jack was an old man. Known to have heart problems."

"Heart problems, maybe," Frobisher sneered, "but

the fact that his skull was split open and there's blood all over a large rock, rather points to something different, don't you think?"

Laurie pulled a face. "Heart attack. Fell, hit his head? All plausible."

Frobisher merely snorted and said he'd see himself out. Which more or less meant that Laurie was right.

A NICE LADY AND A TOMBOLA

It seemed to be a visitor morning at Valley View Farm, for soon after DS Frobisher had left us in peace a lady client of Alf's arrived – an arranged accountancy meeting, so no surprise, and a very nice lady she seemed. Alf introduced her as Nancy Cottingley and she greeted everyone with a bright smile and proffered handshake, gratefully accepted a coffee but declined the offer of lunch, explaining, "I'm meeting a new client at the Oak House Hotel. I believe it's a couple of miles outside the village?"

"It is," Alf assured her. "Rather a posh place, but widely noted for its hospitality and cuisine. Several famous stars stay there for the peace, quiet and R 'n R." He went on to explain, "Nancy is a publishing editor. Jan here, Nancy, is a promising authoress."

I went bright red, expecting the usual response to this statement – which was always: '*What do you write? Romances?*' Too many people assumed that female writers only wrote romances. It was usually a waste of breath to attempt to put them right and enlighten them. However, I was shocked to receive something entirely different when Miss Cottingley asked that customary question, and I'd answered, "Science fiction."

"Oh, that's splendid!" she gushed, clapping her hands enthusiastically. "We desperately need more talented female authors branching out into what has always – annoyingly in my opinion – been taken as a male dominated genre. We women," she went on to say, grasping me by the hand and shaking it vigorously, "are just as capable of writing excellent sci-fi as the men are. I mean, where are more Le Guins, McCaffreys and C. J. Cherryhs? I came across a debut children's book the other day by Tanith Lee. Now, if only she'll get herself off the ground as an adult writer, she'll be an author to watch."

I was pleased, I knew all those authors – apart from Lee. I resolved to look her book up when I got back to work in the library. That was one advantage of being a library assistant – unlimited access to the best books.

Alf disappeared with his client into the private sanctuary of his office and by the onset of the afternoon, Elsie having done all the baking she could (with everything carefully set aside into the safety of her vast larder), she, Laurie and me piled into Alf's car (Laurie driving carefully because of his aches and pains), and headed up the lane to the village hall. We'd been roped into helping to set up the trestle tables ready for the morrow's influx of show entries. I did joke that Aunt Madge and Uncle Toby, by going off to enjoy themselves, had deliberately got out of lending a hand, although it wasn't really 'done' to ask a judge to set everything up, and Uncle Toby was at a disadvantage with his cranky ankle.

Poor Laurie also couldn't help much. He had to step aside from the heavy wooden trestle tables, so was given a sitting down job of sorting out the tickets and prizes for the tombola. Apparently, a Mr Truman, one of the committee lady's husbands, had been allotted to do it, but he hadn't turned up to help. (I overheard Heather remarking that he and his Mrs often thought such chores were beneath their dignity.) Laurie said he didn't mind, but a sedentary job for a man used to action and activity is never easy to swallow. His task involved attaching one of a pair of raffle tickets ending with a five or zero to the many donated prizes with sticky tape, and popping its partner into the wooden tombola drum (and discarding any five or zeros surplus to prize requirements), then adding one of a pair of the remaining raffle tickets to the drum.

Punters would have a rummage inside the drum, pick how many tickets they'd paid for, and if they found a lucky number, would win that prize. Simple to run, a good way to raise funds for charity but tedious to set up, especially as there had been over fifty prizes donated, which varied from bottles of Liebfraumilch, boxes of chocolates, fancy toiletries, jars of honey, chutneys and jams, three boxes of ladies' handkerchiefs and several children's cuddly teddies. Most of the donated prizes were obviously unwanted gifts given for last Christmas or birthdays. (I did laugh, there was even a garden hand trowel and fork set – not donated by Alf, I might add.) I left Laurie to it as I had the job of helping Elsie spread large tablecloths over the trestles as the menfolk erected them in rows down the hall, then to mark out different 'zones' with white tape to separate the forthcoming classes for veg, flowers, cookery and crafts.

Someone had already put up strands of coloured bunting around the hall which made the place seem jolly and festive. I was getting quite excited by the time we'd finished. What with these indoor preparations and the fun and games being organised for the outdoor entertainment on the field next to the hall, Saturday was promising to be a pleasant day. There was to be a tug o' war, a coconut shy, hoopla and a fortune teller's tent, with, for the children, various organised races which were to include a three-legged race, wheelbarrow race, sack race and a frog race. I had no idea what that last one was, but guessed I'd find out.

The congenial atmosphere of anticipated enthusiasm was, however, slightly marred by the chattered speculation about poor Jack Donaldson. Despite what DS Frobisher had insisted, no one thought his death had been deliberate murder. He was elderly – no one knew his exact age, about eighty-five it was thought – and he'd had heart problems. Besides, everyone agreed, who would want to kill harmless, friendly old Jack?

Laurie, being a policeman, was grilled quite a bit for his opinion, but he managed to hold onto a professional stance and respond that we'd all know when an autopsy was concluded, until then everything was just idle gossip.

It was sad, for it seemed that Jack had only one living relative, a nephew who lived somewhere on the Isles of Scilly. Opinion was that he'd inherit Jack's cottage, do it up and sell it on for a fat profit. And that opinion led to further conjecture regarding another cottage in the village, poor Dorothy Clack's lovely little place, which I'd already noticed looked very abandoned and forlorn behind its 'For Sale' sign. Adding fuel to the spreading fire, Dorothy – Dotty Dorothy – *had* been brutally murdered, but her killer had long since been caught and sent to jail, so apart from the matter of an unexpected death, there was no comparison.

I'd liked Dorothy. She was a funny old bird, weird with her belief in different fantasies, but gentle and kindly, her interest focussed on nature. It was a shame that her lovely old cottage hadn't been snapped up by someone nice. The longer it stood there, empty and neglected, the more dejected it looked. I always thought that old houses needed new families to bring them alive again. Perhaps someone would discover it soon and not mind the ghosts, spiders or cobwebs.

_____

8

SUMMER SOIREE SURPRISE

Seven o'clock found us in our glad rags being welcomed to an elegant soirée hosted by Captain Frank Dowd and his wife, Anastasia, who, Laurie assured me, despite her Russian-sounding name was as English as a Kentish apple. They resided at what was fondly known by the villagers as 'The Manor House', although officially it was simply 'End House', being the last house in the village proper. (Discounting all the farms and isolated cottages.)

Standing in three acres of woods and pasture, End House, a lovely Georgian building at the far north end of Chappletawton, had held a grander status in the 1800s, being the home of the village Squire. Neither it nor its residents had ever been of a wealthy Mr Darcy of Pemberley level, but might have been akin to the Bennets of Longbourn – moderately well off, but not excessively so.

Captain Dowd was a rotund, congenial man, but he did rather think of himself as the respected Squire on account of his address, and was, (in his opinion), the most important villager beneath the vicar and the Chair of the Parish Council – except he *was* the

Chairman, so that didn't apply. To his credit, he did sponsor much of the annual Village Show, and had hosted a pre-show thank you 'do' for the committee and noted villagers, such as the members of the Parish Council and their wives, for the past fifteen years.

"Are we allowed to look round the garden?" I asked as we shed our summer coats into the hands of a maid. The day had been warm but rainy, with a damp chill in the air developing now it was approaching early evening. Coats would probably be needed for going home.

"Oh goodness, no!" Elsie exclaimed. "We can wander onto the paved terrace but no further as a matter of etiquette. Inspecting rival entries before the show is strictly out of bounds."

Given that a lot of the villagers had gardens alongside the lanes – or the main village road – which could be clearly seen over the hedges and stone-built walls, this seemed a tad arbitrary, but I let it pass.

After the formal greeting, we were ushered from the entrance hall into a large, elegant living room that was already filled with people.

No one attending the evening party, I soon ascertained, was ungracious enough to even *suggest* that Captain Dowd lived in hopeful expectation of taking the 'best roses in show' silver trophy again this year. The fact that he had done so for several years running was also, tactfully, not mentioned. To be fair, as Alf Walker had told me, the captain's roses *were* beautiful, but Alf had also whispered, "Although he does employ an extremely proficient gardener." Which said it all really, especially as said gardener, Bob Featheridge, did not (tactfully, or because he was an employee?) attend the gathering. As we'd arrived, I had spotted him inspecting a rather splendid rose bed on the far side of some extensive lawns. I knew Mr

Featheridge by sight from previous visits to the village, but had never actually met him. I assumed that he was deciding which roses to pick for his employer to exhibit at the show tomorrow.

All that aside, according to Elsie, the annual Friday Evening Soirée was something the hardworking and dedicated show committee looked forward to.

"It also means," she confided, "that we can keep an eye on each other on the evening before the show, so there can be no sneaking around committing acts of mischievous sabotage."

"Surely not!" I exclaimed, genuinely shocked. Natural annoyances such as slugs, snails and greedy hens were one thing, but deliberate vandalism? In this quiet village?

"Oh you'd be surprised." Elsie elaborated, "Someone a few years back went round the gardens of previous winners spraying highly toxic weed killer everywhere. Captain Dowd's garden looked like the wreck of the *Hesperus*. We never did find the saboteur, but there's been no trouble for several years since then. I think the incident rather shocked everyone, and the show is, really, only meant to be a bit of fun."

I wondered if she was right about the 'fun' bit, because Alf, by contrast, seemed to take his potential entries very seriously. Nor did her 'keep an eye' theory hold much ground, because dastardly deeds were more likely to be committed when everyone was tucked up in bed during the secret early hours, were they not? I stifled a giggle, imagining pyjama-clad villagers sneaking around with torches committing various acts of malicious mischief to each other's lovingly grown marrows, dahlias, roses and tomatoes.

There were a few sorrowful exchanges of general condolence for poor Jack Donaldson's death, but most were tempered with curiosity about any further news.

Was it natural causes or murder? Poor Laurie was rather ear-bashed again about it, but he could only answer with the same response as earlier in the afternoon: that he did not know as this was not his patch, and he knew as much – or as little – as did everyone else. A few people ventured to ask Uncle Toby his opinion, but his standard response was, "Nothing to do with me, I'm on sick leave, thankfully." Which, actually, could have been just as good an excuse for Laurie to use.

Many of the village men present were gathering in an adjoining room where I could see that there was a rather splendid bar shaped like a Spanish Galleon, manned by a tuxedo-dressed professional waiter. Other waiters, similarly clad, circulated to offer wine or champagne, and waitresses attired in black dresses with neat white aprons and lace caps (very 1940s), were starting to circulate with huge silver trays of tempting canapés. This was definitely not your average bright orange plastic bowl of plain crisps or peanuts type of party!

A string quartet was rapturously playing in a large conservatory where the strains of Mozart were currently being drowned by the volume of vigorous conversation. The whole event must have cost a fortune to organise; perhaps Captain Dowd deserved his expected prize for these endeavours? (Although I had a feeling that it was Mrs Captain Dowd who saw to all the organising.)

Aunt Madge was finding herself to be especially popular alongside Beatrice Norbutt/Pye. We soon realised that their apparent celebrity fame was because of their judge status, not their good-natured personalities or witty conversation.

"I'll be a nobody again on Sunday," Beatrice laughed. Which wasn't strictly true, due to her fame as a much loved TV cook, but certainly applied to Aunt Madge, who openly admitted that she was rather enjoying being so generously fêted.

Heather from the shop was chatting to some people I didn't know, but when she saw me and Aunt Madge talking to Beatrice, she grabbed our arms and insisted on introducing us to the other show committee members: Mrs Gillham, Mrs Truman, (the other half of the lazy, anti-tombola Mr Truman), Mrs Mossop, Miss Harbinger and Miss Ansty. The last lady she introduced I recognised by name: Mrs Culpin.

"Are you Mary-Anne's mum?" I asked, ensuring I had a broad smile on my face as I didn't want her to think that I was about to make a complaint about her mischievous daughter. I'd met the girl the previous summer when she'd been teasing various villagers by moving an old scarecrow around. Poor old Dorothy Clack had been a particular target because she was convinced the scarecrow had developed a sentient life of its own. It would have been quite funny, except Dotty Dorothy had been found dead – nothing to do with Mary-Anne or the scarecrow, I might add.

Mrs Culpin laughed. "For my sins, yes, I am her mother. I swear I will go grey well before my time wondering what my little minx will get up to next!"

"Oh, she's not a bad girl," Aunt Madge declared. "She loves life and laughter that's all. Believe me, compared to some of the evil delinquents my husband has to deal with, your Mary-Anne is an absolute angel!"

"I thank you for saying so, but my girlie is definitely no angel!"

"Outside of school I expect there's not a lot for children to do in such a quiet village?" I proffered.

"It's not so bad for the older children," Mrs Culpin agreed. "They can cycle to the railway station or get the bus to Barnstaple or South Molton where there are shops, the cinema, clubs, sports and such. We have the village football and cricket teams, but girls are not allowed to play either, which is a great shame because my Mary-Anne is very good at both."

"You should start a girls' team," Aunt Madge suggested. "All this about what is suitable for boys but not for girls is such nonsense. We girls were quite capable during the war – flying Spits, steering narrowboats on the canals delivering essential supplies, not to mention making munitions. Even our dear Queen was a mechanic!"

"My mother was a train driver for Great Western," Mrs Culpin admitted, "but then, Dad and Grandad were signalmen, so the railways are in our blood. Dad was killed in '42 when a Gerry bombed the line and got a direct hit on the signal box. We lived near Crediton then, and it's that which made Mum decide to sign up for GWR. I was only five, but even at that age I knew enough to be very proud of her. I like your suggestion about starting a girls' team for football and cricket. I might think about it. The Parish Council might back the idea if I approach them."

I knew an anecdote about a wartime incident on the railway from a housebound library reader of mine, and was about to mention it when I became distracted by a group of new arrivals. I recognised the TV celebrity, Rose Carpenter, and what could only be described as her 'entourage', although they seemed embarrassed by her pretentious 'look everyone the star has arrived' attitude as she sashayed into the room as if she were about to receive a Hollywood Oscar.

She was dressed to the nines in a shimmering silver lamé dress with matching stiletto shoes and a silver fox fur cape. (I mean fur? In July?) Diamonds (real or paste?) glittered at her neck, left wrist and on her fingers. Glamour was the intention. Mutton dressed as lamb, the effect. Although this low opinion of mine might have been influenced by the instant ogling of almost every man present, including my Laurie. (Uncle Toby merely raised a single eyebrow. I'm not quite sure if that signified amusement or attraction. I hope, the former.)

Captain Dowd and his wife had moved away from the entrance hall to circulate among their already arrived guests. Seeing the newcomers, he rushed to greet them, and was rewarded by Rose's air kisses to both cheeks. She exchanged a few discreet words with him, waggling red-painted nails at the people with her, presumably introducing them as he shook their hands. Formalities over, her hand apparently glued to the arm of the middle-aged man she'd arrived with, she headed straight for the nearest waiter and glass of champagne. The rest of us were firmly ignored as unimportant. Not that it mattered, for one of her party we already knew – Alf's accountancy client, Nancy Cottingley, and alongside her, to my utter astonishment, the nice young man we'd met at Stonehenge!

We enthusiastically shook hands and exchanged names – he was Eric Dwight Hamilton Junior. "But I'm known as Ed, a corruption of E.D. This is the sort of coincidence you'd not believe if it were in a book!" he laughed as he then introduced us to his sister.

"This is Marianette – but we call her Puppet."

'Puppet' had the grace to blush, but she smiled and greeted us warmly. "I've no idea why Mom called me that made-up name, but I don't mind Puppet, although a lot of the silly remarks get a bit wearing," she said.

"Like 'no strings attached'? I suggested.

"Exactly!" came the laughed response. I liked her. She was only sixteen but her eyes sparkled with genuine and confident fun, which seemed very different from her brother's brief description when we'd met at Stonehenge. I guessed she was a people person, not a prehistoric monument admirer.

"And the gentleman affixed to Miss Carpenter," Nancy Cottingley said in a hushed tone, after saying hello, "is the stepfather of these two delightful young people. And as of this afternoon, he is my latest contracted author."

"Oh, you signed him up then?" Alf beamed. "From what you told me, the thriller novel he's writing based on a TV producer cum amateur detective sounds most intriguing."

"Pa has some incredible anecdotes to use," Ed confirmed. "He's worked on most of the best British TV shows, and he's friends with quite a few actors and actresses."

"And he's worked on the worst shows and made enemies of a few people along the way," Puppet muttered, meaningfully glancing across the room at her stepfather and Rose Carpenter who was continuing to cling to his arm like a desperate, low tide limpet.

"I'd better rescue him," Ed said also peering in their direction. "I've told him all about you lot – he'll be over the moon to know you're here!" With that he went to join his stepfather.

"She's poison," Puppet confided as she lifted a glass of champagne from a tray-wielding waiter. Aunt Madge raised an eyebrow but said nothing. The girl was underage for drinking alcohol, but I'd been allowed a small glass of wine at private parties when I was sixteen, so fair was fair.

"Pa is way too polite to her," Puppet continued. "He panders to her. I've tried warning him several times that she's a right bitch, but he just shrugs and says I'm too young to understand older women." The contemptuous snort which followed adequately summed up the girl's feelings. From the way Rose was behaving, I did rather agree with her analysis as Rose didn't look at all happy about Ed prising away her arm-prop, but Captain Dowd quickly became a suitable substitute. Along with another glass of champagne.

Introductions, handshakes, easy laughter; we found Peter Johnson to be a delightfully witty man who, within minutes, seemed as if we had known him forever. He was fascinated by our chance meeting at Stonehenge, was interested in Uncle Toby's and Laurie's job – genuinely interested, not the polite saying so kind – and was even eager to hear about my work in the library. I initially suspected that most of his conversation would merely be polite, him being well practised at making people feel instantly at ease, a bit like, I suspect, the Queen does when meeting hundreds of new people a week; that knack of making a total stranger feel like an old friend. But no, he seemed totally authentic.

Aunt Madge, I'd noted, had seemed unusually quiet these last few minutes, then she took a figurative deep breath and looking straight at Mr Johnson asked, "Forgive me for being impertinently nosey, but was your wife Susan Hamilton, previously Susan Porter?"

We gaped at her, especially Mr Johnson whose expression was a cross between puzzlement and astonishment.

"Why, yes, yes she was. Did you know her?"

Madge clapped her hands, stepped forward and gave him a resounding hug and a kiss on the cheek – then did the same to Ed and Puppet. "Know her?" She laughed, delighted. "Susan's sister was the mother of Jan here – my husband's sister-in-law! We were there to wave you off, Ed, when you sailed from Southampton to America!"

We all spoke at once:

"Goodness!"

"Well I never!"

"Crikey!"

"Really?"

"Your name, Marianette, and nickname of Puppet, gave the game away, but I did wonder if it was only a coincidence. When you were a baby, Jan and Ed used to play with the mittens Susan insisted you wore because you had long nails, even then, and were forever scratching your own face." Aunt Madge pointed to Puppet's beautifully manicured hands. "The mittens were joined together by a length of wool and these two rascals delighted in using them like puppet strings to make you wave your arms around. I'm afraid the analogy stuck!"

"And if I remember rightly," Uncle Toby added, "Susan came up with the name Marianette, as she'd always admired Queen Marie Antoinette, and loved puppet shows, so she joined the two together, a sort of play on the word *marionette*."

"I prefer Puppet among friends, but my given name will be wonderful for when I become an actress," the girl said with a wide, enthusiastic smile.

"*If* you become an actress," her stepfather interjected, "it will not be until you complete your education and have explored all other possibilities. Acting can be a cut throat business, and I don't think it's for you."

Puppet scowled. I could see this was a family bone of contention, along with Puppet's dislike for Rose Carpenter.

We all hugged again, and I confess I was choking back tears. I loved Aunt Madge and Uncle Toby to the Andromeda Galaxy and back, but outside of them (and now Laurie and the Walkers), I'd not known a family, and all of a sudden I had two cousins!

The only person, that evening, who didn't share in our discovered delight was Rose. Her expression when she heard our news looked like she was sucking on a particularly sour lemon, but then, perhaps for the first time in her life, she was suddenly not the centre of attention?

9

FRIENDS AND FOES

I couldn't remember when I'd last had such a delightful evening. I suppose to be truthful I'd had a wonderful time with Laurie on his birthday back in May, but it had only been a meal at home because my poor boyfriend had been in a lot of pain. He still was, come to that, but he and Uncle Toby had soon found themselves comfortable chairs and both pleading the invalid, were happily ensconced while others attended them. They were like cheerful little kinglings surrounded by loyal courtiers. Everyone understood that sitting was essential for them, but I rather suspected that the opportunity to sit beside them in order to chat was welcomed by many with an aching pair of feet as the evening wore on. Nancy Cottingley and her new client, Peter Johnson, I noticed, had stayed with Alf for much of the evening. Twice I was certain that Peter had deliberately pretended to not notice Rose beckoning him to join her, and once he had politely shooed her away when she'd attempted to intrude on his conversation. Her resulting scowls – accompanied by refilled glasses of champagne – were as evident. She was one seriously annoyed lady with a face as puckered as Grumpy's in Disney's *Snow White*. I began to wonder whether there was some sort of gone-wrong relationship history there? A one-sided admiration which Rose (and Puppet?) had misinterpreted? I mentioned my conjecture to Puppet and Ed, both of whom I spent quite a while chatting to. "Rose doesn't appear to be enjoying herself much," I said.

"Rose Carpenter," Puppet grumbled, "fancies my stepfather, but, thank goodness, the interest is not returned. Pa has better taste. All the same, he ought to make his dislike of her much clearer than he does. Merely avoiding her where he can is not sufficient. He says he's going to get his own back when he writes his novel. The glamorous leading lady will be the victim of a horrendous murder."

Ah.

I noticed that Rose had dropped Frank Dowd and was now closely accompanied by a balding man who wore his faded ginger hair swept sideways across his shiny pate. Mr Truman. What on earth did she see in the oily little man? Apart from the fact he supposedly had lots of money – and excessively flattered her. His wife didn't seem too keen on the attention he was giving the younger woman, though. If looks could kill, daggers would be flying.

Someone else was clearly avoiding Rose; her younger sister, Ivy. I found myself next to her at the buffet table after the first wave of guests had swooped in doing, between them, a good impression of a swarm of locusts. She was surreptitiously peering at the sandwiches to see what the fillings were, saw me and attempted an embarrassed laugh.

"All the little flag labels have been knocked aside," she pointed to the plates of food, "and I'm allergic to salmon and eggs, so I'm looking for the ham or chicken."

"I'm not allergic, but not keen on salmon... here, this dish is chicken. And please don't think I'm being greedy by filling two plates, one is for my fiancé who has to keep off his feet."

She asked why and I explained as she placed four chicken sandwiches on her plate along with three cream cheese vol au vents and a hefty pile of crisps. I guessed she liked her food as, unlike the svelte Rose, Ivy was rather chubby and not as elegantly dressed, and it did not take a Sherlock Holmes to elementarily observe that the two loathed each other. My suspicions were confirmed when Ivy glanced over her shoulder at a loud burst of high-pitched laughter from Rose as she came into the dining room from the terrace, her arm linked through Mr Truman's. They'd both been gone some while, I realised, both had rain-damp shoulders and she had dirt spattered on her shoes and the hem of her dress. He was hastily replacing his lank hair over his baldness. A surreptitious chance for some illicit hanky-panky in the gathering gloom of the garden, I assumed.

Ivy muttered, annoyed. Embarrassed at her sister's behaviour perhaps? "I wish someone would shut her up."

There was nothing tactful I could reply to that, so I pretended not to hear.

"We've only been here two hours and she's drunk already," Ivy complained. "I'll have to drive her home. If she's sick in the car she can clear it up, I'm not doing so again."

I murmured something neutrally sympathetic.

Ivy didn't hear; continued grumbling. "She's mad because the TV show's probably going to be dropped, and that producer isn't as interested in her as she

66

thought. She was hoping that Peter was here to offer her a new contract, but he's been brushing her off and making excuses for weeks now. The ratings have fallen to almost zero for *In Rose's Garden,* and anyone with sense – apart from her with her puffed-up ego – can see she's become a laughing stock among viewers."

I offered more sympathetic noises, but she ignored me and stuffed a sandwich into her mouth.

"Don't feel sorry for her," she said after chewing and swallowing. "My sister is a pain on or off TV. She'll go with any man who has money and flatters her. It's me who does all the gardening, you know. Rose wouldn't dream of chipping those perfect nails of hers, or getting dirty." She laughed, cynically. "Well, not *gardening* dirty. Bedroom dirty is another matter. She only got the job as presenter in the first place because she flaunts her cleavage and went to bed with the original producer. Now Johnson's got lumbered with her. She reads everything about the gardens the show visits from a script written by other people. Wouldn't know a cyclamen from a clematis."

I didn't know the difference either, but that wasn't the point.

Was all this nothing more than jealousy on Ivy's part I wondered? And Puppet's, come to that? Ivy, the unimportant, not very attractive sister, envious of the pretty one? Puppet, the stepdaughter jealous of a threatened new love for the stepfather? I discounted the second. Both Puppet and Ed had said that Peter Johnson didn't like Rose much. So that put paid to *that* theory. Except... where tv and film stars were concerned, they often said one thing and meant entirely another. If Johnson *was* having an affair – producer with lead presenter – neither they, nor the TV company would want such a scandal to be made public. All this stand-offishness could be deliberate pretence. Couldn't it?

There again, I'd probably been over-influenced by reading too many star-studded women's magazines and their exaggerated storylines. And fiction writers are adept at making things up. (OK I wasn't an official fiction writer, but I was determined that one day I would be!)

There came another high, shrill burst of laughter from the other side of the room, and, whatever the truth of my speculation, Rose had definitely consumed too much champagne.

I managed to extricate myself from Ivy's acerbic conversation and delivered the plate of food to Laurie. Did I mention it was his second helping? Being shot had not affected his appetite! I perched on the arm of his chair and ate my own generous helping. That's the only trouble with buffet-type meals, it isn't easy holding a plate in one hand, a drink in the other and be able to eat all at the same time. I solved the problem by putting my half-full glass of red wine on the floor before wading into a very tasty slice of cheese and tomato quiche. (And totally failed to notice that the glass got knocked over. No idea how Anastasia Dowd reacted to a red wine stain on her pale cream carpet when she discovered it. Still, I expect the housemaid knew how to deal with the problem.)

Ivy had cornered her sister and steered her out into the entrance hall where, by the waving of arms and angry expressions, they were clearly arguing. I popped a sweet cherry tomato into my mouth and watched as Ivy threw her arms into the air and stormed off, leaving Rose to stand, slightly swaying, on her own. None of my business I concluded as I selected a cream cheese sandwich. Two bites and a commotion at the open French windows attracted the guests' attention.

The gardener, Bob Featheridge, stepped through from outside, his gnarled, grubby hand clutched firmly around the arm of a squirming girl, who was attempting to kick him, his other hand clutching a small bunch of bedraggled roses.

"Is this vandal's ma 'ere?" Bob shouted angrily, giving Mary-Anne Culpin another rough shake. Everyone was gathering round, even Laurie and Uncle Toby who had both heaved themselves from their chairs.

"I didn't do it! Weren't me!" the girl protested, aiming another hefty kick at the man's shin.

Mrs Culpin retrieved her daughter from the gardener's grasp. "What've you done now, you exasperating child? If you've been up to mischief…"

"Featheridge! Get those muddy boots off my carpet!" Anastasia pushed her way through to the front, angrily pointing at her floor, apparently oblivious to the squirming child or the gardener's annoyance. He did have muddy boots, though, which were leaving their boot print marks (and made me feel better about the spilt wine.)

He was equally oblivious to his employer's wife. "Mischief? Mischief! This wasn't mischief! The little wretch has picked all my roses!"

Captain Dowd harrumphed. "I think they are *my* roses, Bob. But what do you mean?"

Bob brandished his forlorn bouquet. "I mean what I says. Every single rose, bloom and bud from my best bed has been picked and dropped to the ground. Every one of 'em is ruined, and this little blighter did it!"

"I didn't!" Mary-Anne protested again.

"May I?" Uncle Toby asked calmly as he reached out to take the roses. He inspected the poor flowers, their petals already shedding. "These have been neatly cut, not picked, and some while ago for they are already drooping. Secateurs I would imagine. Have you got such an implement, child?"

Mary-Anne's bottom lip was trembling and I guessed that she was choking back tears. "Don't know what sexaters is, sir," she mumbled as a tear slithered down her cheek.

"And why aren't you in bed where you're supposed to be?" Mrs Culpin scolded, giving her daughter another shake. "It's gone ten!"

"I sneaked out," Mary-Anne confessed. "Daddy's watchin' telly an' Gran's soun' asleep. I only wanted to look at all the pretty dresses."

"Huh! Who put you up to ruinin' the roses, eh? Or was it your own idea?" Bob accused.

"No one! I didn't!" Mary-Anne insisted through more tears. Tears of innocence or for being caught red-handed? "Honest, Mummy, I ain't bin near them flowers!"

"Take your shoes off," Laurie ordered, pointing at Mary-Anne's feet and the several distinctive man-sized prints on the carpet. "Let me inspect the soles."

Mary-Anne cuffed her nose on her sleeve, sniffed a few times and stared bewildered at him, but kicked her shoes off. They were a little worn, with scuffed toes. Not her best school shoes, I assumed.

Laurie upended one, held it beneath the nearest wall light, then did the same with the other shoe. "There's some dried mud stuck in the treads, but no wet earth anywhere. Would the child have been able to reach all the blooms without treading on the wet earth?" he asked.

"No, she would not," Mrs Dowd said firmly. "It's raining. The ground will be quite wet. As your boots, Featheridge, clearly show."

"O'course m'boots are muddy," the man protested, "I've been in the bloomin' garden all day!"

Anastasia leapt in. "Precisely. And you're standing on my expensive carpet!"

Uncle Toby seated himself on the nearest chair, told Mary-Anne to put her shoes back on, then beckoned her to stand in front of him. Solemnly he handed her a clean handkerchief. "Now then, Miss Culpin, do you know the penalty for lying to a policeman?"

She nodded, mumbled, "Go to prison?"

"*Mmm*. Go to prison. And you know I am a special, senior policeman?"

She nodded again.

"So tell me the truth, did you damage Captain Dowd's roses?"

Mary-Anne bit her lip and returned Uncle Toby's gaze, straight in the eye. She shook her head. "No, sir, Mummy says not to pick flowers 'cause they soon die, but to leave 'em growin' t'look pretty."

My uncle smiled. "Wipe your nose, sweetheart, and perhaps your mother will be so good as to take you home?"

Mrs Culpin nodded, said goodbye to everyone and left with her errant daughter in tow, who could be heard reiterating her innocence.

Bob Featheridge called after them, "She deserves her backside given a good paddlin'!"

I didn't approve of that. Yes, the girl had been a bit naughty about slipping out of the house at night, but she had only wanted to look. And I believed her about the roses, as, clearly, did Uncle Toby and Laurie. "You have secateurs in your jacket pocket," I observed, pointing to the yellow handles poking out from Featheridge's pocket.

"Of course I 'ave!" he protested, "I'm a gardener!"

"So you could have easily snipped all the roses off," Alf proposed. "Have you, by any chance, entered your *own* roses from your *own* garden for tomorrow's show?"

"No, I ain't," came the indignant reply. Too indignant?

"That's a lie!" Heather blurted out. "I do the entries, so I know you've entered all the rose classes yourself, as well as several of the vegetable categories."

"So what if I 'ave?" Bob blustered. "It ain't agin the rules t'enter me own things."

"It is if you've tried to nobble your main opposition, and cheat wherever you can," someone else I didn't know, insisted. "Are you entering your own roses, Captain Dowd's or poor dead Jack's? You were always in his garden after he'd gone t' bed. Don't deny it, you've been seen often enough."

"Aye, and mebbe you were there when the old boy caught you? Mebbe you did fer 'im? I as reckon we should tell the police!"

"But there's no proof of any of that," Laurie reminded us all. "I agree with DCI Christopher that the girl is innocent of all this. Anyone could have snipped off those roses. Anyone at all. And as far as I'm aware, there's nothing suspicious about old Jack's death. But I'll go look, see if there are any other footprints out there if you like Captain Dowd?"

The captain nodded forlornly. Poor man, he looked utterly stricken as he bent to collect the fallen rose petals. "They were all perfect this morning. Totally perfect."

His bottom lip wobbled. I thought he was going to copy Mary-Anne's streaming tears. I did feel sorry for him, but wasn't happy about Laurie going outside as it was raining, but someone fetched him a large mac and a gentleman's umbrella, and he disappeared for about ten minutes with Bob Featheridge. Came back soggy, but otherwise none the wiser. "Several prints around, nothing conclusive. And nothing of Mary-Anne's size."

Through several hiccups, Rose Carpenter announced, "It's all silly anyway. We all know the winners are the ones who slip the judges the most money."

The room went silent as she lurched crookedly out onto the patio and was violently sick into one of Anastatia Dowd's flower-filled hanging baskets.

10

AN AWKWARD DRIVE

As the clock chimed ten-thirty, the party was over. Several people had already collected their coats, said goodbye, and left. The waiters and waitresses were discreetly clearing the tables and the Spanish Galleon bar had been closed.

"Maybe Ivy had better take her sister home," Anastasia tentatively said, searching the room with her gaze, her lips forming a disapproving tight line. "Oh, is she not here?"

"I think she left a little while ago," Heather said, then whispered to Aunt Madge, in the sort of whisper that would have carried for miles even on a soft breeze, "Every year Rose gets herself well and truly pickled. I don't know why people think she's so marvellous."

Mrs Truman, I thought, certainly didn't think that. She and her husband, I realised, had also gone – with a flea in his ear, I wondered, or was Mrs T used to his outrageous flirting with a younger, prettier, girl? I made a bet with myself that they'd be 'having words' once in the privacy of their own home!

"I'm afraid most sensible people don't think that at all," remarked Peter Johnson from behind us, partially confirming my thoughts. "It isn't public knowledge yet, but the TV company is dropping the show, thank goodness. They're not going to renew Rose's contract because there's been too many complaints about her behaviour from various people – wives mostly – and she is very difficult to work with, even when she's sober. I was given the task of telling her the bad news."

"I presume she took it badly?" Laurie assessed.

Peter shrugged slowly and ruefully shook his head. "Alas, I still haven't plucked up courage to tell her. I've rather been hoping she'd realise it herself, or some sort of fate would intervene for me."

"Someone should shoot her and put us out of our misery," Puppet muttered under her breath, although I think I was the only one who heard.

I had every sympathy with her and Peter. I'd only met Rose Carpenter this evening, but could tell that she was a very obstructive – and destructive – person. I met her sort all the time in the library. Pompous, rude, men and women who thought they owned you and the world owed them.

I recall one woman I'd served. She'd handed me her library ticket and the card which stated a book she'd reserved was beneath the counter for her. I found the book, removed its pink slip with her name written on it, stamped the return date and handed it to her with a smile. "Here you are Mrs Mainwaring." Except I'd said it like it looks. Main Waring.

"It is pronounced 'mannering'. Do you not possess a single intelligent brain cell? I assume you are one of these Secondary Modern School girls who had no value in receiving an education or learning correct English."

I'd managed to maintain a dignified silence and a fixed smile. A pity that library assistants are not allowed to throw books at people.

"Is there anyone who could take Rose home?"

Anastasia asked hopefully expecting someone to volunteer. No one did.

Laurie sighed. Ever gallant, offered, "We came in two cars, neither I nor the DCI fancying squeezing ourselves into one – and neither of us able to walk, even though it's not far. I'll drive Miss Carpenter home."

"And I'd better come with you," I added, "in case she needs help of any sort."

"She'd better not be sick in my car," Alf muttered, echoing Ivy's earlier doubt.

Laurie grinned. "I'll hang her out the window, Dad."

We said our goodbyes and hugged our new-found relatives – their next stop was Cornwall and they were leaving straight after breakfast which was a shame, but they promised to keep in touch.

I was surprised that Nancy Cottingley also gave me a hug, and said something about meeting up again soon, but then she was a nice lady, and was being ultra polite. Everyone said this sort of thing but never actually meant them. Look at holiday friendships, the promises made, never kept.

It took a bit of manhandling – womanhandling – to manoeuvre Rose into the front seat of the car. (We figured the front was better than the back.) Fortunately, she slept for the short journey, but the problems started when we reached our destination. Her home and the gardens of her 'estate' were not far outside the village. We turned in through some open gates onto a long drive but I couldn't see much of the gardens as it wasn't light enough to see more than greyness and dark shadows. The house, when we reached it, had only one light on, a low voltage porch lantern. I got out of the car to save Laurie struggling – Rose was still asleep – and bashed on the front door. No answer. I bashed again and a light came on upstairs followed by a window opening and a head peering out.

"What? Who is it?"

I recognised Ivy's outline and her voice. "It's me, Jan Christopher. We've brought your sister home. I'm afraid she's rather the worse for wear."

"Huh, nothing unusual about that! Wait a minute, I'll be down."

I did wonder just how she had expected her sister to get home, but figured this situation was a common occurrence and Ivy relied on some mug to oblige.

Ivy appeared wearing a pair of old, worn, slippers, faded Bugs Bunny pyjamas and a patched gentleman's dressing gown. "I'd gone to bed," she grumbled as, between us, we dragged Rose, who had finally, but groggily, woken up, from the car.

"Do you need help getting her upstairs to bed or anything?" I asked, willing Ivy to say no.

A young man appeared at the door. He too was dressed for bed and cuddled a toy rabbit. I reckoned he must have been in his early twenties?

"I woked up," he said, stuffing a thumb in his mouth.

"Yes dear. Go back to bed," Ivy said with what I took to be forced patience.

"Is Rose poorly?" he asked, not moving an inch, clutching his rabbit tighter.

"This is Ollie, our brother," Ivy flapped one hand roughly in his direction. "Father named him Oleander for his favourite plant, but no one else has ever called him that. We've all got plant names. I hate mine, Ollie hates his, although he's too stupid in the head to know anything anyway. Brain damaged at birth. I'm stuck with looking after him since Mother buggered off somewhere with someone, and Father died soon after."

"Doesn't Rose help?" I asked as I watched Ivy

trundle her inebriated sister towards the door as if she were a heavy, rusty old milk churn.

Ivy merely laughed, somewhat caustically.

"Did you water the greenhouse?" Rose slurred, stopping dead in front of the porch and putting a hand out onto an ivy-clad trellis to support herself, while pointing another finger at her brother. "I bet you didn't. You're too stupid to do anything useful round here."

"I used the hose when you were out," Ollie said with a grin. "It went 'whoosh' and made fairy rainbows."

"You couldn't water a bloody pond," Rose snapped. "Did you turn the tap off, after? I bet you didn't do that, either."

Ivy tried again to steer her sister indoors.

Rose ignored the pushing and pulling and started to walk off in the opposite direction, her high heels scrunching on the gravel. "I'll check the Idiot has turned the hose off. You know he isn't reliable."

Ivy protested. "He's making it up. I watered before we went to that stupid party."

"Are you sure I can't help in any way?" Laurie asked, watching Rose as she wove unsteadily in the direction of a greenhouse hidden by a stand of conifer trees.

I wasn't having that. We would not be helping with anything, I'd already noticed that he was starting to feel pangs of discomfort, and I had a feeling this exchange of annoyance between the sisters was about to erupt into a full-fledged argument.

"We'd better get going," I hissed, and climbed into the passenger seat. "Get in Laurie, let's leave them to it." He hesitated a second or so, but as the abuse grew louder, he nodded agreement, got into the car, started the engine and performed a perfect three-point turn.

In the wing mirror I could see Ivy following in

Rose's wake. Ollie stood beside the open front door, a look of stark bewilderment on his face. He waved to us, then trotted off after his two sisters.

As we turned onto the lane, we narrowly missed a black car, the driver wrongly assuming there was enough room in the lane for both of us.

"Imbecile," Laurie muttered. I wasn't sure if he meant poor Ollie or the car driver.

I was relieved to be heading for home. There were far better ways to end what had, otherwise, been a pleasant evening, and hanging around to witness a family brawl was not one of them. Besides, I'd realised during the short drive that I'd left my manuscript in Alf's office. I knew he always locked the door at night and I wanted to retrieve it before going to bed.

11

CUCUMBER CONUNDRUM

SATURDAY 28TH JULY 1973

What with one thing and another, I didn't get my pile of typed paper. First, we all sat drinking coffee, (I know, coffee at bedtime? Probably not a good idea, but…) discussing the evening, our new-found relatives, Rose Carpenter's unpleasantness and her sister's dislike of her, and wondering who had cut those roses.

"My money's on Bob Featheridge," Elsie said with a firm nod. "He always enters his own roses, but never wins because Captain Dowd does."

"The same applies to several other villagers, dear," Alf pointed out. "Truman. Heather's husband, Dan Mossop. Ralph, our neighbour from down the hill. Me. And my roses are superb this year. I'm sure I'd win if it wasn't for Dowd."

Laurie guffawed. "You'd better be careful, Dad, Featheridge will be accusing you of the sabotage if he hears your boasting."

Alf chuckled. "That he will. Especially when I do win!"

Now, that's what I call confidence!

Aunt Madge observed, "Without proof, there's

nothing anyone can do about Dowd's roses. You can't exactly take fingerprints from a rose, can you?"

"Oh you'd be surprised where fingerprints can be found nowadays," Laurie replied, "but it wouldn't prove anything. Bob probably handled those roses many times, assessing which ones Captain Dowd should enter into the show, and who knows who else has walked round that garden being nosey?"

"Or maybe Mrs Dowd is the culprit?" I suggested. "Fed up with her husband boasting about the roses, or embarrassed about his wins." I giggled, it was totally irrelevant but I added (out of mischief), "and are we sure she isn't a Russian spy?"

"She was born in Guildford, I believe," Alf said.

"That doesn't make her *not* a spy!" Laurie laughed.

Elsie sniffed disdainfully. "Personally, I think we should change the rules so that everyone has to be responsible for growing their own entries. The captain's a nice man but hasn't done a day's gardening in his life. Featheridge does it all for him."

"Neither has Rose Carpenter by the sound of it," I said. "Ivy says she hasn't a clue about gardening. For TV she reads from scripts written by other people."

Alf nodded. "She's right. Ivy looks after that place of theirs, she's the real gardener. Rose just takes all the credit when in front of a camera."

The topic changed to what entries Alf was going to submit, but we were interrupted by Bess barking at the door.

"What's the matter, girl? Want to go out for a wee?" Laurie said, getting to his feet.

"She went out as soon as we got home," Elsie contradicted. "Hang on! There's a torch light in the garden… look! It's reflecting on the greenhouse glass!"

Laurie and Uncle Toby couldn't run, but we let Bess

out and she shot off up the garden, still barking wildly with Alf in hot pursuit, and us ladies – me, Madge and Elsie, hurtling behind.

There came some shouting along with the barking and the sound of feet haring off up the lane, then a car driving off at speed.

"Did you see who it was?"

"Anything damaged?"

"Be quiet Bess!" (That was Elsie.)

Laurie arrived, torch in hand, which he flashed around the greenhouse – the door was open, despite Alf assuring us that he had shut it before we'd left for the party.

"Nothing damaged or touched by the look of it… ah, no, some blighter's nicked all my cucumbers!"

There was the evidence, two tall, healthy cucumber plants with not a full-grown cucumber attached.

"My cucumbers!" Alf wailed. "Three in particular I had earmarked for tomorrow. They were perfect!"

"Today," Uncle Toby corrected, glancing at his watch. "It's gone half-past twelve, you know."

"Can't we take casts of footprints or something?" Elsie said, indicating for Laurie to shine his torch on the concrete floor.

"There's one faint possibility," he answered, peering at the ground, "but it's indistinct, and we can't very well go asking the entire village to show us their boots, can we?"

"It was a man, I think," Uncle Toby said, "dressed in black with a woolly hat. Could have been anyone."

I could see that Alf was annoyed, but he shrugged and was philosophical about it. "I didn't stand much chance with my cucumbers anyway. It's my peas and roses I've got hopes for."

We trooped back to the house. I was exhausted, it had been a long, eventful day. I noticed Elsie smile as she shone the torch on two enormous purplish-blue hydrangea bushes. "They're all right at least," she announced with a satisfied nod, although I'm not sure how she could see them clearly in the dark, even with her torch.

12

INTERLUDE: LAURIE

It seemed that the household was up and about at the crack of dawn, although actually, I heard first movement at just gone seven. I got up, half-heartedly attempted some of the muscle-strengthening exercises I was supposed to do, and went to the window to study the view across the valley. A view I would never tire of, the greens and yellows of the rolling, grassy or crop-growing hills – barley, wheat, maize. Trees of every possible shade; the meandering river in the distance. I watched two buzzards lazily circling against the grey morning sky, their mewing evocative as they called to each other. I reckoned it would rain before long. Two roe deer were grazing in one of the fields lower down the hill. Dad wouldn't be too pleased if they ventured into his garden! We'd had a magnificent Red Deer stag in that field one winter. He'd looked magnificent against the deep, moonlit snow. He'd come down from Exmoor in search of food. Next morning we put hay out for him near the hedge, and saw him browsing there several times that week. The Red Deer really are magnificent and we felt privileged to quietly watch this Prince of Exmoor from an upstairs window. He disappeared when the snow melted.

I enjoyed London, enjoyed (on the whole) my job, but London wasn't a patch on Devon. Idly, as I stood there watching the day come alive, I wondered how Jan would feel if I suggested we moved here after we were married, then dismissed the idea. A rural policeman wasn't in the same league as one based in a London suburb, even as a Detective Sergeant. That's why I moved out in the first place... but... But, I did love Devon. Jan would never leave Madge and Toby, so there was no point in even thinking about the idea. I smiled to myself: it really was hard for me to think of my boss as 'Toby', but we'd agreed it was to be that at home and DCI Christopher in public. It would be even stranger to call him 'Uncle' after my marriage!

I suppose I'd better confess that Jan and I slept together now; we were engaged, after all, and we had sought permission from both sets of parents.

Back in Chingford, Madge had insisted on converting a couple of their upstairs rooms into a bed-sit for us with our own bathroom, bedroom and sitting room, though we shared the kitchen. Far more comfortable than the dismal section house where I had previously been quartered, and it meant I could put more of my wages away to save for our own, eventual, house.

My parents had replaced the single bed in the large end bedroom here at home with a new double, and both sets had given their blessing as long as we were 'sensible', which meant adequate precautions. Dad had hit the nail on the head with his realistic remark of, "You can get a girl just as pregnant with a quick-sneaked tumble on the sofa, so you might as well be open and sensible about it."

And Madge had let slip that she and the only love

of her life (DCI Christopher) hadn't been married when they 'got together.' Although she had also added that their relationship had blossomed during the height of the war when *Carpe Diem* was the general opinion. 'Seize the day'.

"Back then, we were constantly aware that tomorrow might not come," she had said. I could understand what she meant. It must have been awful to see loved ones go off to war, never knowing if they would come back, or even if they did, whether they would be the same person. A lot of them, for one reason or another, weren't.

Jan was still sound asleep, buried beneath the eiderdown. I could see Mum and Dad in the garden, pondering which flowers to cut and present for the show. I waved when Mum looked up. It was best, I knew from past years, to select flowers in the morning when they were fresh with dew. Mum had her wicker trug on her arm and I could see it was already quite full. I hoped Dad's cabbages had survived the night without too many starving slugs and snails getting fat and doing their worst. As to who the cucumber thief had been, we'd have no way of finding out. One cucumber looked very much like another.

I went downstairs to make tea, found Madge already in the kitchen, one step ahead of me.

"I thought I'd make myself useful," she said. "Your mother has already sorted out what scones, jar of jam and the best Victoria Sponge to take to the show. She's selecting her flowers now. It's all very exciting, isn't it?"

I laughed. "It is, but it's also nerve wracking. I saw Mum in the garden, and I can guarantee that she will be stressing over which hydrangeas to cut. She's won that class two years running. Dad will be pondering whether his peas are plump, if his beetroots are perfectly round, his sticks of rhubarb are straight enough and whether his onions are the size of small footballs. Show day, believe me, is stress day."

Madge grinned. "But it *is* all just for fun, right?"

"Oh yes, just for fun – apart from the serious rivalry about winning Best In Show and the grumbling about the uselessness of the judges."

"Oh, right. Thanks for that unequivocal vote of confidence, Laurie!"

13

SHOW DAY!

Elsie and Alf set off before us in their car, which was packed to the gunnels with boxes, pots of plants and flowers, jars, cakes and crafts. I had a list of their entries which I'd ticked off as each had been carefully loaded into the car, minus the cucumbers and the tomatoes that had stubbornly remained unripe.

Vegetables, Fruit and Flowers
   10 pods peas
   2 heads cabbage
   3 beetroots globe or round
   3 onions grown from seed
   ~~2 cucumbers~~
   ~~3 salad tomatoes~~
   3 sticks rhubarb
   6 raspberries (unstalked) on a glass dish
   4 strawberries (unstalked) on a glass dish
   3 gooseberries on a glass dish
   12 sweet peas, any colour, any variety
   4 dahlias, any variety except cactus
   3 hydrangea heads in a vase

4 roses, any variety

1 specimen rose (with leaves)

6 pansies

A flower and foliage arrangement in an unusual container

(Elsie had cleverly tucked a jam jar inside a wellington boot, and arranged lots of tall flowers, including gladioli, sweet williams, those big, white daisies, stocks and delphiniums. The effect was quite good.)

A colourful hanging basket

Domestic and Handicrafts

a pot of strawberry jam

a pot of chutney (labelled)

3 scones with a small pot of jam (no cream)

a 7-inch Victoria Sponge

a teddy bear dressed in a knitted costume as a character from a book

(label naming character and book)

an embroidered cushion cover depicting nature

Dairy

4 hens' eggs, white

4 hens' eggs, brown

The teddy was my very own Bee Bear, dressed by Elsie as a Cavalier from *The Children of the New Forest* by Captain Marryat. He – Bee Bear, not Captain Marryat – looked very swish in his leather-look (light brown wool) surcoat, red cummerbund, black breeches and boots, silver (knitted) sword at his side and a huge feather in his (knitted) Cavalier's hat. We hoped that all other entries would be predictable things like pirates, Cinderella, clowns and such. The cushion cover Elsie had embroidered – she'd started it at Christmas – was beautiful, depicting autumn-coloured trees with two deer in a meadow grazing beside a bubbling brook, while three geese flew against the early rays of a setting sun. It was stunning.

The eggs we were extremely careful with, putting them gently into a small basket lined with straw – *scrambled* eggs were not on the schedule!

Aunt Madge, in order to be as strictly fair as possible and not glimpse any of the entries, had taken herself off to have a bath and then dress as a respected judge should dress. (Elegant grey suit and a fetching straw hat bedecked with silk flowers.) She'd worn a similar hat when judging classes at a Chingford horse show the previous summer. That one'd had real flowers which one of the winning horses had promptly eaten. Fortunately, Aunt Madge had seen the funny side of the incident.

The rest of us followed about twenty minutes later in Uncle Toby's car – too far for our invalids to walk. The village carpark was busy with show entrants taking their prize specimens into the village hall. I assisted one elderly lady with her heavy box of pots and jars as she was struggling with them and a walking stick – she was most grateful and kept calling me 'Janet dear'. I hadn't the heart to tell her that my name wasn't Janet.

Aunt Madge declared that she'd not enter the hall until it was time to close the doors and begin the judging, in order to not see any entries before they were being shown in all their glory, so she and Uncle Toby opted to take a walk through the village, claiming there were, "One or two things we want to look at."

Inside, I was gobsmacked. The usually somewhat

drab, wooden-walled hall looked absolutely beautiful! There were the several rows of trestle tables running the length of the hall and covered in pristine navy-blue cloths. Individual areas had been carefully marked out with white tape for each class, with little flags stating each class number and description, with most of the tables already groaning under the weight of entries. The colours were incredible, the smell of flowers, fresh fruit and veg intoxicating. Competitors were displaying their entries with explicit care: making sure the flower arrangements were just right; the carrots, runner beans and rhubarb laid down perfectly straight. The crafts set to best advantage; the cakes and scones temptingly arranged on fancy plates, and jars of preserve displayed as per the rules. My Bee Bear sat proudly amongst a little array of – as we'd hoped – predictable characters, although the one dressed as Dracula was pretty good.

Alf beckoned us over to where he was ensuring his cabbages were displayed correctly. "There are seven entries for cucumbers," he whispered. "I'm certain that two of them are mine."

Laurie laughed. "Dad, all cucumbers look exactly alike. There's no way you can tell one from another."

"I know my own stuff," Alf muttered, but said no more.

"Should that dear little snail be hiding in the middle of this cabbage?" I asked. I'd never seen Alf move so fast as he ran to inspect the offending item!

"You're a mischief maker!" he declared when he realised I was joking.

On the stage was an arrangement of two vertical step ladders and a horizontal one that had been erected to hold the display of hanging baskets. This was, Elsie had explained, a new category this year, so was uncharted territory for the displayers.

I helped her hang her two entries – both were heavy and a mass of frothy fountains of red, white and blue trailing blooms. Mission completed, I threaded my arm through one of the ladder's steps and pretended to hug it.

"This is not my real ladder, I didn't know my real ladder. This is my step ladder."

She laughed outright at my punned joke.

Heather heard and chuckled as well, but was having difficulty because her display was even heavier than Elsie's and Heather was shorter, so couldn't reach the horizontal bars that easily. I stepped in (excuse the pun again!) to assist. I was pleased that she'd laughed because she looked somewhat frazzled.

"Thank you dear, it has been one of *those* mornings so far! I had two baskets entered but someone had tampered with one during the night. Deliberately snapped the chain, so everything had spilled out. My poor little flowers are quite ruined."

"Was that the basket with the bent chain?" Elsie queried. "I pointed it out to you the other day, I said it had a weak link so ought to be checked."

"I did check it, and it seemed all right to me. Someone deliberately broke it, I'm certain." Heather glared at Elsie. Was she accusing *her* of the deed? Surely not, they were best friends.

"Who would do that sort of thing? To what gain?" I declared, feeling anger rise up inside me, although I wasn't sure if that was because someone might be cheating or Heather seemed to suspect Elsie of foul play. How did cheating help anyone? If it made them win, where was the pleasure in knowing they'd done so by deliberate mischief?

I'd had the same experience in the ring when showing horses. Judges looked for perfectly turned-out riders and horses: clean tack, gleaming coats for the horses, spotless clothes for the riders – which included total cleanliness on the soles of boots. (I'd seen doting mamas lift their dear children onto the pony then remove the plastic bags covering the feet.) The animal's mane and tail had to be neatly plaited. Now, I was hopeless at this, my plaits were never of a uniform size – some pea-sized, others like golf balls – and several invariably fell out half-way round the show ring. Aunt Madge had always maintained that I had to turn my pony out myself, though, otherwise what was the point of taking part? Which I did agree with, but other competitors (snotty posh kids) all seemed to employ professional grooms who could plait blindfolded, in the dark, with one hand tied behind their back. Honestly, was a Red Rosette really worth all that effort? Needless to say, the only time I won First Place was once when I was the only one in the class. I didn't really care if my pony, Rosie, was a scruffy, fat little Welsh Mountain urchin. I loved her and that was all that mattered.

Heather was, however, quite cross. "We have no way of knowing who the perpetrator – or perpetrators – are. If I get my hands on her I'll not answer to the consequences."

"Or him? It could be a he, not a she." I told her about the person Alf had seen running away in the early hours.

"We've never had this sort of thing before," Heather said, shaking her head, "but there are several new people in the village now. Outcomers. I expect they don't understand the meaning of *friendly* rivalry." She stopped talking and her face flushed bright red. "Oh, Jan dear, I didn't mean to offend! You'll not be classed as an outcomer because you're marrying Laurie, nor will your aunt and uncle if they decide to buy Meadow View."

I stared at her. Didn't know what to say for a long moment. "Sorry?" I eventually stammered, "what do you mean 'buy Meadow View'?"

"Dorothy Clack's cottage, the one up the road from here that's for sale. Your aunt is very interested in buying it. I hold the key; she's having a good look round as we speak."

I stared at her. That was news to me!

14

FIDDLING WITH ONIONS

Heather's bombshell – unintentionally uttered, I was certain – had to take a backstep, as she and Elsie were urgently called to the hall's entrance lobby on committee business.

I caught up with Alf and Laurie who were fiddling with ensuring the onions were facing 'best side out'. (They seemed the same all round to me!)

"Did you know anything about Meadow View?" I asked them, in what I hoped was an innocent tone.

"Dotty's old place?" Alf said, giving one onion another quarter turn to the front then turning it back again. "Been up for sale for months now. People get put off as soon as they discover a murder was committed there. Heather's a lovely, dear person, but she does tend to chatter and let cats out of bags."

"I suspect," Laurie volunteered, "that she does that deliberately, a sort of test to see if the right people are suitable as prospective villagers."

"No," I persisted, "I meant did you know anything about Aunt Madge and Uncle Toby wanting to buy it?"

That must have stunned Alf as much as it did Laurie, for he stopped twiddling his onions.

"Just looking out of interest, perhaps?" Laurie offered. "They're surely not thinking of moving down here? Are they?"

I shook my head. Were they? If they were would I mind? Crikey, yes, I would! Where would Laurie and I live for a start!

All thoughts and speculation were thrust aside, though, as Elsie hurried up. "There's a problem," she panted. "We close the doors to the public in five minutes so the judges can start judging, but Rose Carpenter is not here. Heather is plying Beatrice and Madge with coffee and cake in the side room, but Rose should have been here fifteen minutes ago."

Ah, I thought, *so Aunt Madge has finished her house hunting then?*

"Won't plying with coffee and cake be seen by some as bribing the judges?" Laurie suggested, grinning.

"Don't be silly," Elsie reprimanded. "It's only coffee and cake."

"No £1 notes slipped under the saucers then, as Rose implied yesterday?"

I couldn't resist adding, stifling a giggle, "Or tucked in the hanging baskets?"

"Be serious both of you. We need Rose Carpenter here. Now."

"I'll take the car and fetch her," Alf offered.

"You can't, you're wanted over on the field opposite to help set up the stalls in the marquee for this afternoon. And Mrs Lofts needs a strong man to assist with the boxes of books for her second-hand book stall."

Laurie sighed. "That's you nabbed then Dad. I'll go see what's happened to Rose. Got the car keys?"

Alf fished in his jacket pocket and tossed a bunch of keys to his son. "Don't scratch the paintwork. Rose's lane is even more of a goat track than ours is."

Laurie grinned. "Coming with me Jan?"

The last thing I wanted was to meet with Rose Carpenter again – especially as setting up a book stall was far more appealing – but loyalty to one's beloved took priority. Unfortunately.

15

WHERE'S THE JUDGE?

We talked about nothing in particular as Laurie drove: how pretty the lanes were in their array of summer wild flowers, how big the spring-born lambs had grown to, the ridiculously long, gangly legs of a foal we spotted in a field; speculated on the age of two enormous oak trees which stood as bookend sentinel guards at the start of a farm lane. At one bendy and narrow point, Laurie had to reverse (competently, I might add), to the nearest passing place so that a tractor towing a trailer loaded with sheep could get by. "Moving them to fresh pasture, I expect," he said. "There's too much traffic nowadays to walk them along the lanes."

"Too many impatient drivers," I agreed. "No one is prepared to dawdle along behind a flock of sheep."

I thought back to last summer when traffic along the main road from South Molton had to wait for about five minutes while a herd of cattle was moved from their field on one side of the road to the farm on the other side for milking. This happened twice a day, morning and evening, there and back again but I'd found the whole experience utterly wonderful. To watch those solemn cows amble along in front of us with no intention of hurrying or troubling themselves was far more interesting and entertaining than having to wait at red traffic lights as we did in town. I was reminded, as I'd watched, of that poem, *Leisure* by Welshman W.H. Davies:

> *What is this life if, full of care,*
> *We have no time to stand and stare.*
> *No time to stand beneath the boughs*
> *And stare as long as sheep or cows.*

Mind you, the road itself was in rather a mucky state after all sixty of them had crossed!

Laurie switched the windscreen wipers on for the rain was now more than the slight drizzle it had been earlier. I hoped it wouldn't last long – rain wouldn't be good for the outdoor events. We exchanged not a word about Dotty Dorothy's cottage. I wasn't even certain whether Laurie knew anything about my aunt and uncle being interested in buying it. I was about to broach the subject when he announced: "This is the place. I suspect she's nursing a whopper of a hangover."

He turned in through the open wrought iron gates set within a high stone wall. I wondered whether we should have closed them last night, but Laurie said he'd never seen them shut, so assumed not.

"I don't suppose they can be bothered to keep getting in and out of the car to open and close them," he stated.

I agreed. We had gates to our house in Chingford, and they were a pain. I was often on about investing in automatic gates, but Uncle Toby always retorted that such things were enormously expensive. But then it was rarely *him* who had to get in and out to open or close them.

I hadn't been able to see anything of Rose's place last night, it being too dark. The drive was quite long and twisting flanked by iron-railed fields where sheep grazed, a small woodland and then lawn and shrubberies to each side. We rounded a bend and there was the house, which I'd assumed would be quite grand and posh, but, on the contrary, appeared neglected and in desperate need of some T.L.C. (Or at least a coat of paint over the flaking window frames, and the white-limed walls, which were distinctly shabby.)

We parked up and I got out, went to the porched front door and bashed on the knocker just as I had last night. No answer. I knocked again, and as before, heard a window opening from somewhere above me. I stepped back outside and, hands on hips, stared up at the tousled head of Ivy Carpenter.

"Hello. We're looking for Rose," I called.

"She'll be at the village show," Ivy called back.

"No, she isn't. No one's seen her."

Ivy said something unrepeatable, followed by, "I'll kill her if she's still asleep in bed."

She disappeared, was gone for several minutes, then I heard the bolt being drawn back from the front door. Ivy opened it, stood there in the patched dressing gown and Bugs Bunny pyjamas. "She's not in her room, and her bed hasn't been slept in."

"Did you see her go to her room last night?" I asked as neutrally as I could. There was definitely no love lost between these two sisters.

"No. She was being exceptionally grouchy – as I have no doubt you heard – so I left her out here to stew and took myself to bed. I'm not her babysitter."

Was that crossness in her voice, or worry? Or, I couldn't help thinking, guilt?

"I'll take a look round," Laurie said from behind me.

Ivy disappeared back indoors, shutting the front door and not inviting me in, which I thought was extremely rude. Not wanting to be left standing like a lemon I followed in Laurie's wake. He was staring at a huge pond, more of a mini lake really. Much of it was overgrown with rushes and reeds, but there were quite a few rather attractive water lilies.

"What's that out there?" Laurie asked, pointing to something floating near the centre. I couldn't see what it was, but it looked ominous. "I wonder how deep this is?" He asked rhetorically. He found a stick and started poking into the water.

"There's a boat over there." I pointed to one side where there was a small apology for a wooden landing stage and a dinghy tied alongside.

"Oh good, I wasn't looking forward to having to swim."

I did sometimes wonder whether my fiancé was mentally stable or a complete idiot. No one in his (or her) right mind would even *think* about swimming in that water – apart from the fact it was green and scummy, all those reeds and stalks and roots and tendrils would make it extremely unsafe. I wasn't sure that even a boat would be able to get far. I was reminded of a scene in another of my favourite children's books, *Swallows and Amazons*, where the children were rowing *Swallow* up the Amazon river (not the real Amazon, the story is set in England's Lake District), then got stuck in a huge patch of water lilies.

We walked round to the jetty, inspected the boat. It had several inches of water slopping about in the bottom, no oars, and looked distinctly rotten.

"I don't think the boat's a good idea," I said.

"Boat not good," repeated a voice behind us, and we spun round to see the brother, Ollie, coming towards us at a sort of shuffling waddle. "Bad. Boat broke. Not allowed in boat. Be in trouble to get in boat," he announced, emphatically.

Thanks for the obvious, I thought, getting worried as Laurie was slipping off his jacket.

"Do you know what that is, floating in the pond?" I asked Ollie, pointing.

"Weeds," came the answer.

"No, that big thing in the middle?" *Keep calm and patient*, I thought to myself.

"A tree. Fell into the water many sleeps ago."

That was a relief; it wasn't Rose, then. Laurie put his jacket back on. "I don't suppose you know where your sister is, do you?" he asked.

"In bed. Ivy is always in bed 'til the cuckoo clock cuckoos ten cuckoos."

I smiled at the boy... no, he was a man, not a boy. He was fully dressed but I could see pyjama bottoms under his shabby old trousers, and he had odd socks on. His shirt was mis-buttoned. If someone usually helped him to dress, they hadn't done so this morning. "No, not Ivy. We mean Rose. Do you know where Rose is?"

Ollie smiled and nodded vigorously, pleased to be of help. "Yes."

Patience, Jan, patience! "Oh that's good. Where is she, then?"

"Asleep. She's been swimming. Not good swimming without a swimming cozzie!"

I exchanged glances with Laurie. Swimming? Perhaps that wasn't a fallen tree after all?

"Where did Rose go swimming, Ollie?" I asked.

"In the greenhouse. I'm hungry. Want my breakfast."

Not the pond, that was a relief, but what did he mean by 'in the greenhouse'? I exchanged puzzled looks with Laurie. He raised an eyebrow, shrugged, indicating that he had no idea what Ollie had meant.

Ollie toddled off in the direction of the house, in pursuit of food, I assumed.

"We'd better investigate," Laurie said.

We walked quickly towards where we could see a large – but as shabby as the house – greenhouse behind a stand of conifer trees. The door was wide open and water was trickling out, not deep, but enough to make us paddle through where it had formed puddles. The swimming reference became tragically clear.

We found Rose lying face down on the flooded concrete walkway between two long rows of raised beds of pink, white and red carnations.

Wound around her neck was the hose that had been spouting water, but now only dripped feebly. It had been running for hours by the look of it, but someone had now turned it off. Ollie perhaps?

It wouldn't have been Rose. She was quite dead.

16

BAD NEWS

I ran to the house intent on fetching Ivy, but also to call the police as a priority, and then try to contact someone at the village. Heather would be frantic about where their judge was, although I guessed that Aunt Madge and Beatrice, between them, would sort something out. Rose's death might have been an accident, but from the way she was lying, and the fact that the top of her skull was split open, I somehow doubted it.

I raised my hand to knock on the house door, but it swung open to reveal a furious Ivy still wearing her pyjamas and dressing gown.

"That damned idiot brother of mine," she complained, "has run the bloody well dry. There's no water."

Ah, that possibly accounted for all the flooding. "The hose was on in the greenhouse, it hadn't been turned off," I said. A mundane thing to say, unimportant compared to the other, tragic, news that I had to impart, but a good excuse not to talk about what I ought to have been talking about. "It's only dripping now, but there's water everywhere, so it's probably been on all night and run your borehole down to below the pump level."

Lots of farms had boreholes. Often on bigger properties, more than one. Laurie had told me about Valley View Farm's borehole on my first visit to Devon. Fresh, clean water which was pumped up from an underground aquifer beneath the water table that could produce a limitless – to a degree – amount of water. The limit was the depth of the pump set to bring the water up to the installed water tank. If the level fell to below the pump, there'd be no water until the level rose again. Usually, running dry was not a problem when there was adequate rainfall, but a nuisance in a long, dry summer – or if someone left a tap or hose running. Forgetting to turn a tap off was something you only did once because of the inconvenient consequences.

Ivy, however, was not interested in details so I didn't mention them. "Which one of my siblings was so damned stupid?" she complained. "The idiot brother or the thoughtless, drunk, sister? They're both as unreliable as each other. I need a bath. And coffee. Bloody useless, the pair of them. Honest I could kill them at times. I swear I'll swing for them one of these days…"

I held my hand up, palm outermost in order to stop her from incriminating herself any further.

"Ivy, Rose is dead. It looks like there's been an accident. Where is your phone? I need to call the police."

17

INTERLUDE: LAURIE

Needless to say, it had to be DS Frobisher who (eventually) turned up, strolling in, hands thrust into pockets, as if he were joining a casual summer picnic party not attending a murder scene. Uniform had arrived fairly sharpish, along with an ambulance crew – not that they were needed, too late for first aid, or last aid, come to that, but such a crew was all part of the expected procedure. SOCO had arrived too. The original Scene of Crime Officers, or Crime Scene Investigators (CSI), were involved in basic crime investigation during the late nineteenth century when fingerprinting became a specific technology, with CID handling what was required. The dedicated civilian roles, the SOCO team, came into being in 1969 and were now widely used, although some CID personnel resented the change. I can't think why. The specialised equipment, experience and knowledge these SOCO people possessed far outweighed what we, ordinary policemen, could use, and their involvement left us free to do the other side of crime investigation – catching criminals and using our 'little grey cells' as Poirot would put it.

The other advantage of SOCO, they usually worked as an established team. Not saying CID were not a team, but our personnel were known to change as often as the tide turned. I was lucky that I seemed to be on a long-term association with DCI Christopher. (Although he often remarked that he was 'stuck' with me!) And in this instance, here in Devon, I was relieved that the SOCO team had arrived and immediately got on with their work, because DS Frobisher was, not to mince words, useless.

This was obviously murder without motive. Rose still had all her jewellery in place, the bracelets, rings and necklace. So robbery was out. The very top of Rose's skull had been bashed in by something heavy, and that hose had been wrapped round her neck *after* she'd fallen. Or so I assessed – an assumption confirmed by the head of the SOCO team, Dave Gortman. Nice chap, mid-forties, bald, very knowledgeable. There were no overhead beams to have caused the skull damage, and if she'd fallen or tripped, such an injury would have been to the front, side or back of the head, not the crown – unless she'd fallen from a height, head first, which I knew had happened to blokes like jockeys, telegraph pole engineers, builders, roof-menders, parachute jumpers and such.

Frobisher's first remark when he arrived, even before seeing the crime scene, had been: "Topped herself has she? I'm not surprised, she's bloody awful on TV."

Idiot.

———

SOCO found patches of blood at the side of the walkway, soaked into cracks, but much of it had washed away with the running water. Not that there was a lot of blood anyway. There were bits of jellyish sort of stuff in places, which I didn't investigate. Scattered brain matter is not particularly appealing. And anyway, like I've said, this was not, would not, be my case, so I left that particular 'pleasure' to Frobisher.

Before he, or anyone, had arrived, Ivy had come running up from the house, dressing gown and old slippers flapping. She was in a state, shock mostly, but it all overflowed when she saw the body, although I tried my best to stop her going into the greenhouse. She was one strong lady, and I backed down because I didn't fancy being punched in the midriff, or anywhere else, come to that. Besides, her fingerprints, footprints, wisps of hair, spots of blood – whatever – would have been everywhere anyway, I expect she'd been in and out of this greenhouse almost every day of her life since she'd been able to toddle. Her scream at seeing the body was awful, poor woman, and she crumpled to her knees, despite all the puddled water. I managed to get her up and steered her outside, where she promptly vomited into a bush of something or other. (It had pretty little purple flowers – no idea what it was. Lavender? Although it didn't smell like lavender.)

I've seen many a body in my time as a policeman – as a uniformed copper and as a detective. You get to see the most gruesome things that one human can, deliberately, or accidentally, do to another. Murder was gut-wrenching and I'd thrown up on more than one occasion. It was the callous indifference inflicted on what had once been a living person that got to you, especially where savage revenge or rage had been involved. The unmeditated 'losing it' and lashing out, resulting in a life destroyed was one thing, pre-meditated set out to deliberately murder, another matter entirely, though both had the same consequences. More than just the unfortunate victim's life shattered. Families were destroyed, too, the parents, siblings, grandparents, aunts, uncles, cousins, all suffered whether they were related to the dead person or the murderer. Life, when it fell apart because of violence, was not an easy thing to endure.

Death by accident was as bad. RTAs – Road Traffic Accidents – in particular, especially where drink or dangerous driving was concerned. And children.

All of it hurt.

"Who'd do such a thing?" Ivy gulped after she'd calmed a little and I'd made her sit down on a low wall. "Who so badly wanted her dead to do this?"

I assumed the questions were rhetorical. I had no answers to offer. Not beyond the obvious that she would be the prime suspect, but it wasn't my place to say anything.

"Shouldn't we cover her up, or move her somewhere more… more dignified?" Ivy asked.

I shook my head. "No, I'm afraid this now constitutes a crime scene, the less it's disturbed the better."

Ivy nodded, understanding what I was getting at. "She wasn't liked much," she said with a small, accepting sigh. "The village despised her, and that TV chap couldn't stand her. He might have had good reason to bump her off."

"You mean Peter Johnson?" I asked.

She nodded. "*Mmm.* Rose had her claws well stuck into him. An unmarried man with money? This place…" she haphazardly waved one hand, "is like a bottomless pit. The more you shovel into it the more it swallows up. We're nigh on bankrupt, you know. Rose was counting on another TV series, but Johnson wanted to get rid of her. The show's a flop, Rose is probably the worst TV person ever." Ivy paused, gulped. "*Was* the worst."

Several questions popped into my head – I was a good detective, so of course they did, but not only wasn't it my place to ask them, did I *want* to ask them? Get involved? Which in itself was worrying. Was I losing interest in policing? A job I thought I loved?

It didn't matter because Ivy more or less answered them without me asking.

"Those kids of his. They hate her too. Can't say I blame them. They could see her for what she is – was. A gold-digging bitch."

Ivy looked up at me and shrugged. "It's the truth, I don't – didn't – like her either. Bossy cow that she is – was. I'd not want her dead though, without her this place, my home, is as dead as she is. I was born here, you know. Everything comes to me after she's gone. Not that I want it."

"Not to your brother?" I queried. Most estates and businesses such as this one passed to sons, not daughters, even if the daughters were older.

Ivy laughed, a sort of gurgling cackle. "Ollie? My idiot brother Oleander? The one who's as thick as two short planks? The one who pisses his pants because he forgets to go to the toilet? That moron? Inherit this pile of rubble and dung? Don't make me laugh, mate!"

Well, that told me, didn't it?

"What did you mean by Mr Johnson's children not liking her?" Habit. I couldn't keep my mouth shut, could I?

"They've been here several times. Easter, Bank Holidays and such. Occasions when the TV have been filming in the gardens. Believe it or not, this place over the back, beyond the pond, is quite lovely. Well, at least, it looks lovely on TV if you've got a decent cameraman who knows how to angle a lens properly. There's a summerhouse the other side of the woods, they did a lot of filming in there on wet days. Least, that's what Rose claimed. I'm more inclined to believe she used it for other things. Never could keep her knickers on where men were concerned."

To my great relief, Jan appeared, whispered that the police and others were on their way. "I phoned the village shop, too. They'll pass a message to Heather. All I said was that Rose was indisposed. Was that the right thing to do?"

I gave her a quick, pecked kiss on the cheek. Yes, the right thing to do.

Jan was very good with Ivy, too. Putting her arms round her she persuaded the distraught woman to walk back to the house – her intention helped along by a new, light, drizzle of rain.

The rain caused a slight problem. Did I wait outside the greenhouse and get wet, or did I shelter just inside? A prick of conscience decision – inside meant I could be the one messing up evidence, but then, I decided, I'd already been inside so one more footprint wouldn't make much difference. I left uniform in charge as soon as they arrived and made my way to the house, where I found Ollie seated at the kitchen table eating a bowl of cornflakes.

"There's no tea," he stated as I entered. "No water in the tap."

"Well's dry," Jan stated, knowing I'd know what she meant.

Ivy was not there. I asked where she was.

"Upstairs, getting dressed," Jan answered, but at that moment Ivy entered the kitchen. Her face was pale, eyes red-rimmed.

She must have heard us talking, for, as she slumped into a chair opposite her brother, said, "There's emergency water in the carry-bottle under the sink. You know that, Ollie, why didn't you tell them? You're such a useless mutt." She glared at him as I went to the cupboard she'd indicated, fetched out a large plastic bottle of water, the type used by campers.

Ivy smiled at me. A weak smile, but still a smile. It was good that she was making the effort. "I'd die for a cuppa…" she remarked, then realised what she'd said and gulped down more tears.

I filled the kettle and set it on the Aga.

"Rose went swimming," Ollie said, repeating his earlier claim. "Got her dress wet. Father will be cross."

"Oh shut up, you stupid idiot." Ivy snapped. "Father's dead, Rose is dead, can't you get that into your empty, stupid head?"

We sat in silence around the table, each nursing our own thoughts, the only sounds, Ollie crunching his cornflakes and the kettle starting to sing. It occurred to me that Ollie had been in the greenhouse. Had he touched, or moved the body? Did I ask him – or keep quiet and leave such questions to whoever arrived from Barnstaple Police?

"She *is* swimming, I sawed her laying in the water!" Ollie insisted, stuffing another spoonful of cornflakes into his mouth. After a couple of chews, said, with his mouth full, "I pushed her 'cause she squitted me with the hose. I hit her, *thwack*, and pushed her over. The water was cold. Serve her right."

Jan and I looked at him, horrified.

Ivy got up, the kettle was boiling. She spooned tea leaves into the teapot, then poured water in. "That was years ago, Ollie," she said with a sigh. "We were children and she was tormenting you. She was always tormenting you. Us."

I looked at Jan, she looked at me. I shrugged. The words were noted, but this was not my case, was it?

"What did you hit her with, Ollie?" I asked.

"Dunno. Something. I laughed at the blood on her dress. Served her right for being snotty."

Ivy, I could see, was clenching her fists and teeth. "I've just said, that was years ago, so shut up." She looked at me, blinking back tears. "He gets muddled. Has no idea of time or events. Rose always said he should have been drowned at birth. There's times that I agree with her."

"You can drown when swimming," Ollie added, sounding quite cheerful. "I can't swim, but Rose can. I hit her and she went swimming in the water. Got her dress wet."

"Oh, for God's sake! You keep saying that, the police will assume you killed her, you moron." Ivy thumped her palm onto the table, stood up and went out of the room. We could hear her footsteps on the stairs, and then a door slam.

I had to tell Frobisher, when he eventually arrived. And I knew that he would immediately bark up the wrong tree. He knocked at the house and I escorted him up to the greenhouse, filling him in with what little I knew and what Ivy had said. Not that he was appreciative, or even appeared interested. As predicted, as soon as I related what Ollie had said, Frobisher jumped to the conclusion that the lad was the culprit, a belief enhanced when Dave Gortman filled us in with some preliminary observations.

"Hit from above. One blow, we think by a brick. That one there, probably." He pointed to a brick that had already been bagged to be taken away for examination. "It has something which could be blood, bone and brain matter on it. I'll know more after detailed analysis. Death more or less instant. Hose put round her neck after death. No bruising to see, so not strangulation. A joke, perhaps?"

"So, hit by someone taller than her?" Frobisher asked. "Someone tall enough to whack her one?"

"She could have been kneeling or bending," I suggested.

"The imbecile is our likely suspect. He's tall, what, over six foot, I'd say. The sister, Ivy? She's only mid-five foot?"

"Or Rose could have been kneeling," I said again.

"It's a possibility," Gortman confirmed. "But kneeling in this fancy party frock of hers? Come to that, why was she watering a greenhouse dressed like this anyway?"

"She was drunk," I explained. "Jan and I brought her home from a party in the village, dropped her off, left her outside the house with her sister, Ivy."

"And…?" Frobisher mocked. "What then?"

I shrugged. "We drove off. The two women were arguing, then the brother appeared and…"

"So he was involved. My money's still on him."

"We'll know more when we've had a good look," Gortman emphasised.

Frobisher half-sneered and mouthed the words: *when we've had a good look.* "Don't you ever know things straight off?" he mocked. One of the CID who resented the specialist work, then. Like I said. Idiot.

Frobisher gave orders that Uniform were to take Ollie Carpenter in for questioning. I queried whether Ivy was to be taken in as well, but Frobisher, in his wisdom, didn't see the point. "You've already told me that the numbskull has admitted pushing and hitting Rose. What more do I need?"

"But Ivy said that was years ago."

Frobisher laughed at my protest. "Course she did. Covering for him, isn't she?"

I tried again. "Ivy has motive. She inherits this entire place if Rose is out of the way."

Frobisher shrugged, not listening.

I didn't agree with him, but let it go. Hoped Ivy had

access to a decent lawyer for her brother. If she bothered to get one, which I had a sick feeling she wouldn't. "What about that other incident?" I asked Frobisher as we walked back to our cars. "In the village, the old boy, Jack Donaldson?"

"What about him?"

"An update?" I could see Jan in the kitchen, tapped on the window and beckoned her outside. Time for us to go, to leave Frobisher to it.

"Nothing official yet," he said, "but it seems it was natural causes. Heart attack. He keeled over, cut his head open then his heart stopped ticking."

Exactly as I'd already suggested.

"So your father and his trowel are in the clear."

That was something, I suppose.

"And Ivy?" I pressed again as I got into the car with Jan.

Frobisher shrugged. "If it keeps your lordship happy, I'll take her in for questioning. Waste of police time. I'll let them know at the station it was your idea."

Again. Idiot.

18

FUTURE, FUN, AND GAMES

As I had expected, the judges had very quickly re-organised themselves. Laurie popped into the hall to give a brief outline of what had happened to Rose, but it was agreed to keep quiet and not make any public announcements. There was nothing that could be done for Rose Carpenter, nor Ivy or Ollie, come to that, and besides, Ivy had specifically asked us not to say anything for as long as we could. After all, it wasn't as if a serial murderer was on the loose. Keeping quiet was in everyone's interest.

Laurie and I tried to set the unpleasant events aside and enter into the spirit of the village afternoon. The drizzly rain had stopped by noon, and the entire village – and beyond – had turned out to enjoy the additional entertainments set out on the field next to the hall, and to visit the food marquee where vegetables, flowers, crafts and homemade cakes and pastries were on sale alongside bric-a-brac stalls and other fund-raising ideas. Each stallholder was entitled to keep what profit he or she made, with a 10% donation going to the Village Charity Fund. (The village had a different, local, charity each year, and usually gave a substantial donation.) I, naturally, had a browse of the bookstall where I picked up a couple of bargains for myself and three travel guides which I thought Alf would like.

We also couldn't resist the fortune teller's tent, although Laurie had pointed out that the 'fortune teller' was only Joyce Renford from the village dressed in her gypsy costume, but as I hadn't a clue who she was it didn't matter. (As it turned out, I did recognise her, as she was one of the barmaids at the Exeter Inn.) According to her crystal ball, Laurie and I would have a long and happy life together and to expect some surprising news. Which wasn't really fortune telling just clever guesses.

As for the hall, the doors would not open until 3.30 p.m. when all the judging was finished, the judges had eaten their provided lunch, and the sports on the field had been completed. Although Aunt Madge later said that after sampling various Victoria Sponges, scones, gingerbread biscuits and whatnot, as well as teaspoon-tasters of jams and chutneys, she hadn't wanted such a big Ploughman's Lunch. But the cups of tea had been well received.

The tombola that Laurie had helped to prepare was proving popular. We had three goes each, winning, between us, a box of dog biscuits (Bess would be pleased), a box of sugar lumps (Aunt Madge's horses would be pleased), and a silk scarf. (I was pleased!)

By the time the various sports started Laurie and I had cheered up a little. The next village along, King's Nympton, won the tug o'war with their beefy team, and I discovered what the frog race was. Children competed by hopping or jumping like frogs from a start line to a finish line. It looked great fun, but terribly energetic. I was pleased that Mary-Anne Culpin won the girls' over-tens race. She might get up to mischief now and then, but was a good kid at heart.

An egg-and-spoon for adults was about to take place when Laurie and I were surprised by an unexpected "Hello!" and a hand clamping onto my shoulder. I spun round, startled.

"Ed!" I squeaked, "what are you doing here, I thought you were off to Cornwall first thing this morning?" Pleased to see him, I gave my new-found cousin an enthusiastic hug.

"That was the plan," he said, "but things went awry when we got back to the hotel last night. My incredibly clever sister – a bit tipsy we suspect – tripped up the hotel steps, fell, and cut her head open. A nasty cut, so Pa had to take her to the emergency room – casualty – at the hospital."

That didn't sound too good. "Is Puppet OK?"

"She's fine; a few stitches, but as it was a head injury they kept her in overnight. On the way back, though, Pa ran out of gas – petrol." Ed laughed at himself. "I need to get out of this awful habit of using Americanisms, don't I?"

"We've all run out more than once," Laurie acknowledged. "They used to have petrol pumps outside the Exeter Inn, but they've gone now. The trick is to never let your tank go below half full."

Ed nodded, taking in the good advice. "Pa managed to coast for a short distance, but then realised he was on the lane which runs past Rose's place – he recognised that old dead tree near there, the one that's sticking two fingers up to the world. Do you know the tree I mean?"

We did. Knew it well. Laurie had driven me that way several times especially so we could laugh at nature's joke. It was a tree that had been blasted by lightning years ago, leaving two bare, gnarled, thin trunks pointing up from the main trunk looking much like a clenched hand making a Harvey Smith V sign with its two 'fingers'. The tree had become a cherished landmark for the locals who didn't care for Rose Carpenter, so summed up their general feeling against her.

(And for those who don't remember the British showjumper's gesture from his win at the All England Showjumping Course, Hickstead, Sussex, in the summer of 1971, his impromptu V sign was a spontaneous reaction when he won a prestigious event two years running, but hadn't been expected to. The gesture was soon dubbed by the press as 'doing a Harvey Smith'; a blunt Yorkshireman, the sort of rider you either loved or couldn't stand. Me? I admired his riding ability.)

"It was about 1 a.m. by then, so he pushed the car into Rose's drive, and went up to the house to explain, with the vague idea of either calling the Automobile Association for their new twenty-four-hour breakdown service, or begging a lift back to the hotel."

"Do AA patrol men still have to salute members when they see them on the road?" I asked, unintentionally diverting the conversation, but genuinely curious.

Laurie answered as Ed had no idea. "No, that stopped sometime in the '60s. The original idea was to respectfully acknowledge members, thus encouraging drivers to join the AA. *Not* saluting turned into a surreptitious warning code about police speed traps. If a patrolman *didn't* salute, a driver was entitled to pull over and ask why he'd not been acknowledged, resulting in a carefully worded explanation about a speed trap further on up the road. Very clever, and completely legal."

Interesting, but I had interrupted Ed's tale.

"He knocked at the door a couple of times, but no one answered, so he gave up and decided to walk instead."

"Not easy in the dark without a torch," Laurie offered.

"Oh, Pa's one of the practical kind, he always has a flashlight in the car. Anyway, he walked, though he was damned cross that he did try to flag a passing car down, but the driver ignored him and sped off."

"That was mean, especially at that time of night," I said.

"The hotel obliged with a can of Go Juice and a ride – lift – early this morning, so Pa got the car and went straight into town to fill up and fetch Puppet. She has a wonderful black eye as well as six stitches and a splitting headache, so Pa decided to pack her off back to bed, postpone Cornwall and stay over until tomorrow. The hotel is being very obliging, seeing as it was a loose slab on their steps which caused Puppet to trip."

Laurie frowned. "That's unlike the hotel to be so lax."

Ed grinned. "There's no proof the blame can be put on the hotel or the steps, but it's amazing what can be achieved by a bit of bluff." He half-shrugged, half-laughed. "That's not the end of it, though. A jackass of a policeman arrived and demanded to see Pa." Ed stopped, blushed slightly, "Oh, apologies Laurie, I meant no disrespect."

"None taken," Laurie answered dryly. He'd been called far worse than a 'jackass' on more than one occasion. "Would the jackass, by chance, go by the name of DS Frobisher?"

Ed looked surprised. "He did. Do you know him?"

Laurie's response remained dry. "Unfortunately, yes."

"Anyway, absolutely absurdly, this Frobisher wanted Pa to answer some questions. Something about an incident at Rose's place? As Pa had been there... It seemed Ivy *had* heard him knocking but had completely ignored him. Not very friendly, but not unexpected, given the nature of that dysfunctional family. Well, this DS of yours wouldn't tell us anymore than that, just hauled Pa off to the manager's office and kept him there for half-an-hour. I don't suppose you know anything about all this do you?" To his credit, Ed blushed. "I guess I'd better confess. I came here specifically to ask that question. Hoped you could shed some light? Pa's as perplexed as I am."

"Not really, I'm afraid. It's not my case, nor my place..." Laurie began, but Ed jumped on his words.

"Not your case? Something *has* happened then? Jeez. What's Pa got mixed up in with that bloody awful woman now?"

"Which one? Do you mean Ivy or Rose? They both seem as bad as each other, in different ways." I murmured before I realised I'd said it aloud.

Ed sighed, stuffed his hands into his jacket pockets. "I think I mean both. I don't know Ivy really, but we've met two or three times when Puppet and I have been with Pa when they've been shooting that bad TV show. Ivy's convinced that Pa's having an affair with Rose – I assure you, he isn't. He doesn't like either of them. But Ivy's got it into her head that Rose is going to marry him, and Pa'll then have ownership of Rose Gardens. Why he'd want to be saddled with someone like Rose, or own what amounts to a neglected garden centre is beyond me, but there you go. Puppet thinks that Ivy's got the hots for Pa herself, which is why she's so jealous. I'm inclined to agree with Sis. Frankly, we'd be better off with the lot of them dumped and out of our life."

A huge cheer resounded from the playing field. The children's egg and spoon had been won by a delighted Mary-Anne Culpin. She was doing well with her sporting wins today. And a minute or so after the last race the grey sky turned blacker and rain poured down.

Everyone made a dash for the village hall.

19

WINNERS AND LOSERS

It couldn't have been better timing. The sports had finished, many of the stalls had sold out of whatever they were selling, the refreshment tent had no more cakes left, Gypsy Joyce had put her crystal ball away, and the judges had finished judging. With the rain falling, the main doors were flung open and eager competitors and their families crowded in to the hall to discover how their entries had fared. The excitement of anticipation was electric.

Peter Johnson turned up with Puppet on his arm – poor girl, her face was spectacularly bruised; she'd certainly come down a wallop. On the plus side, they'd decided to stay on even longer, until Monday at least, so Elsie invited them to Valley View to join us on the morrow for Sunday lunch.

We were agog to hear what had happened with DS Frobisher, but Peter wasn't able to say much more than it had all been a misunderstanding, and he'd explain later, where and when it was less public. Which was frustrating, but understandable, especially as Rose's death was still not public knowledge.

We inspected 'our' entries laid out so beautifully on

the trestle tables, grinning broadly at each one that bore a prize certificate.

Alf was delighted. His beetroots and onions had been awarded second, his roses, peas and fruit had all been placed first – so a triumph even without the stolen cucumbers and abandoned tomatoes. His dahlias, pansies and sweet peas came third along with Elsie's cushion cover. (I think she deserved second, if not first, but the two entries which beat her were also quite marvellous.) Her jam and chutney came nowhere, alas, although she hadn't expected to do well in those categories, but her Wellington Boot arrangement had been awarded first prize along with her hydrangeas, scones and Victoria Sponge. Her hanging basket came second, and we were pleased to discover that Heather's lovely display had taken first place. Though I did hear someone unsportingly muttering that as Heather had plied the judges with coffee and chocolate cake before the judging had commenced, what was so surprising about the result? Bribery was implied. Totally unfairly, as it was Heather's job to look after the judges. Some people can be so silly! (On reflection, I did wonder if the comment had been intended as nothing more than good-natured banter.)

To my delight, Elsie also came first with Bee Bear's outfit.

Once all the speeches and 'thank yous' had finished, the trophy giving drew lots of applause for the winners. Mary-Anne received a trophy for best girls' sports, and Alf's face was a picture of beaming pride as he went up to the stage at the far end of the hall to receive three trophies for his veg, fruit and roses, and then as the last announcement, one for overall Best In Show. He couldn't resist making a short speech, thanking the committee for organising such a wonderful show, to the judges for their expert judging, and, "I must add that to whoever stole my cucumbers, it was rather a waste of time, as I've still been awarded this handsome trophy. Maybe you'd be advised to pick my peas next time, if you can get there before my wife's hens, or the snails do their worst?" Everyone laughed.

Several people during the day had mentioned suspicions of mischief-making, and there was quite a bit of speculation about who had cut Captain Dowd's roses. He had gallantly attended the show, but had only gained second or third places for his few entries. His roses, all knew, were his great pride and joy, and the expressions of condolence and 'better luck next year', did not make up for their demise. No one, thank goodness, was unkind enough to suggest that Alf had nobbled the captain's roses, even though he'd won the trophy. The gardener, Bob Featheridge, I noticed, hadn't entered anything after all. In fact I hadn't seen him all day.

So, the Village Flower and Vegetable Show 1973, was all over. The marquee, stalls and refreshment and fortune teller's tents were about to be taken down, and the exhibitors were collecting their items, some joyfully, others attempting to conceal disappointment.

Mary-Anne Culpin was buzzing with pleasure as she showed us her trophy and rosettes, and could barely contain herself for a special 'Best in Category' that she'd been awarded for her children's flower arrangement – an arrangement with a difference. The category was, 'Any flower exhibit arranged in a 7-inch round baking tin, to represent a holiday'. Mary-Anne had been very innovative. She'd chosen Christmas as her theme, using holly sprigs and ivy, and a plastic Father Christmas on his sleigh, along with a robin and a Christmas tree that her mum used to decorate their annual Christmas cake. The innovation? She hadn't used *flowers* - but *flour* to create snow, with her label reading, 'A Merry Floury Christmas.' Aunt Madge and Beatrice had roared with laughter, hence the special Best in Category award.

Thrilled, Mary-Anne collected her exhibit and swung round to show me and Laurie. "The flour makes good snow, don't it!" she beamed.

Behind us, collecting his own exhibits, Mr Truman stepped backwards, bumped into Mary-Anne and sent her cake tin flying. Flour went everywhere.

"Bloody kids!" he shouted, unaware that it had been his fault, not Mary-Anne's. He scooped up a pot plant (that hadn't won anything), and marched off, not even bothering to apologise or offer to help clear up the mess. (And there was rather a mess, as you can imagine.)

To my surprise, Laurie told me to stand aside, keep still and hobbled off at a hobbledy-dee run in pursuit of Mr Truman.

"Truman," he shouted, "just you wait there, I want a word!"

Everyone in the hall turned to look. Truman hesitated, thrust his pot plant into the arms of a startled Heather and made a dash for the door. Unfortunately for him, Uncle Toby and Aunt Madge were right in his path. My uncle stuck out his walking stick and tripped the fleeing man up. As a flourish, Laurie twirled his own walking stick and rather like a conjuror, twisted the handle to withdraw a very impressive rapier which he waved near the felled Mr Truman's throat. I knew that walking stick was really a gentleman's swordstick, but Laurie rarely showed its true nature in public and had told me to keep its secret firmly to myself. Policemen, he'd maintained, shouldn't walk around with dangerous weapons even if, technically, the weapon is no longer sharp. But revealing it had a great effect on Mr Truman.

"I think we've found our mischief-maker," Laurie announced to the intrigued people packed into the hall. "Can you explain, Mr Truman, why your very distinctive shoe print was imprinted on Captain Dowd's rose beds, was clearly marked in my father's greenhouse and now, is very plainly showing in young Mary-Anne's spilled flour? Perhaps as well," Laurie added with stern policeman's authority, "you could enlighten me as to why you were seen in the close vicinity of Rose Carpenter's home on one definite and one possible occasion last night? Your car nearly collided with mine, and Mr Johnson has informed Barnstaple Constabulary of a partially recalled number plate. Yours perhaps?"

Naturally, Mr Truman could provide no innocent explanation.

Mary-Anne Culpin had been staring wide-eyed at Laurie and Mr Truman. Quite a bit of the flour had fallen on her skirt, socks and shoes. "Mummy will kill me," she whispered through quivering lips, tears pricking her eyes. "These were clean on this mornin'." Then her gaze hardened and she pointed a (none too clean) finger at Truman. "I saw you!" she announced. "In Captain Dowd's garden las' night. You were picking his roses and giving them to Rose Carpenter in between patting her bum and kissin' 'er." She screwed up her nose and mouth in an expression of disgust. "It was all very yucky!"

Truman managed to push Laurie's blade aside and scrabble to his feet. His face was beetroot red with fury. "All lies!" he shouted, "I'll sue you all for such libel!"

"I think you mean slander," I corrected.

"Huh! There's no slander about it!" An equally enraged woman pushed her way through the gathered crowd. Mrs Truman. "You, Peregrine Truman are a cheat, a liar and a slimy toad. Don't think I don't know what you've been up to, cavorting with that slut, Rose Carpenter behind my back, sneaking off to her house after dark to have some sordid how's-your-father with her. Hoping she'd return your attentions by giving you first prizes today. Well, that didn't work out did it, you stupid man."

Everyone gasped as she grabbed a particularly cream-filled Victoria Sponge from the trestle table beside her and upended it right onto her husband's bald head. Dignified, she turned on her heel and strode from the hall, leaving with the parting words, "Don't bother coming home. I want a divorce."

Interestingly, the entire crowd was silent for a few seconds then, as one, burst into a round of approving applause.

20

HAPPY BUT TIRED

Exhausted, we returned to Valley View after the show as happy people. Rumour had spread by the end of the show about why Rose Carpenter hadn't turned up, but although the committee had been informed, it had been generally agreed that until the police made an official announcement it was not up to anyone to say anything. The rumours were way off the mark, the majority of speculative suggestions assuming she had a hangover and wouldn't surface until dusk, like a vampire. We had, however, held a minute's silence for poor old, much respected, Jack Donaldson before the prizes had been handed out.

Further speculation ceased, we heard (from Heather), the next morning when word had got out, that Rose Carpenter had been found dead. The police had taken Truman in for questioning and, we also heard, had kept him at the police station overnight until he could summon a solicitor. (At least he had a bed for the night, if not a very comfortable one!) There was no doubt that he had been behind all the flower show mischief, Alf now being certain that he'd been the one to raid his compost heap and steal his cucumbers.

Hardly a police matter, though, in comparison to being suspected of murder, but even that suspicion was dropped for lack of evidence and proof. Truman could hardly deny his affair with Rose Carpenter, but he had been cleared of murdering her.

(He didn't get away so lightly with Mrs Truman, who true to her word, divorced him, took every penny he had in alimony and moved to Clacton-On-Sea where she opened an efficient B & B business.)

All in all Saturday had been a good day, the only thing to mar it, I couldn't find my novel. Alf assured me that it was safe in his office. "Locked away with my papers." I hadn't the heart to beg him to go and look that evening, it might have been a good day, but a tiring one.

Aunt Madge confessed to being exhausted, and asked us all to remind her, next year, not to agree to being a judge. "Not unless," she joked, "the committee provide spare new feet. Mine are killing me!"

"You might not be invited as a judge again," I said. "Who's to say we'll be in Devon next July? Unless you're thinking of moving here?"

Aunt Madge had the good grace to flush pink.

"Ah. Who told you about Meadow View?"

"Heather."

Elsie laughed. "That sounds about right, Heather is an absolute darling, but is hopeless at keeping secrets."

"To be fair," Aunt Madge countered, "it isn't a secret. Yes, Toby and I had a good look round the cottage, and we've put an offer in. But..." she held up a hand to stop me interrupting, "but we have no intention of moving just yet. It'll be a holiday cottage for us until Toby decides to retire – and *then* we'll move here. So you've quite a few years to wait."

I must say, that was a huge relief!

The grown-ups (as I was tending to affectionately

call them all), trooped off to bed by ten o'clock, leaving Laurie and me to snuggle together (with Bess and my prize-winning Bee Bear), on the sofa. Laurie said he had a surprise to share. (I hoped it was my missing manuscript, but it wasn't.) Curiously, he turned on Alf's stereogram.

"I came across this LP in town last week. It was released back in May, but is still fairly unknown. It's instrumental, unusual. Starts with a repeating riff, and piano sequence, then uses different instruments dubbed together and more or less played by the same person. He's fantastic. I've never heard anything like it before. But what do you think?"

I sat and listened, not having a clue as to what a 'repeating riff' was, but soon found out. By the last track on side one I was transfixed: each instrument was announced, one by one by some chap I didn't know (but had a super voice), as if he were a master of ceremonies announcing guests arriving at a grand party. The final 'guest' was the musical equivalent of the icing on the cake.

"Plus... Tubular Bells."

A perfect end to what, all in all, despite everything, had turned out to be an enjoyable village show day.

21

HOW IT ENDED

Some things turn out well, some things don't. We all had to wait patiently for Sunday to discover more news of what exactly had happened. Laurie annoyed me by sleeping in late and dawdling when he did finally get up. Aunt Madge and Uncle Toby went to have another viewing of Meadow View Cottage. I admit, I was excited about the prospect, and Laurie, when we'd eventually got to bed, had hinted that maybe moving back to Devon sooner, rather than later, might be a good thing. Except, he'd fallen asleep before we could talk more.

The aroma of roast beef, Yorkshire Pudding, roast potatoes and all the usual trimmings for Sunday Lunch filled the house – along with apple crumble and cream for pudding, so that we were all salivating by the time Peter Johnson, Ed and Puppet arrived at 12.30.

Gradually the story of everything that had happened came out as we sat in the Walkers' dining room tucking into our lunch. DS Frobisher had questioned Peter because Ivy had stated that he'd been at the house in the early hours of Saturday morning.

(Thus annoying Peter even more because she'd ignored him.)

"It didn't matter how many times I told Frobisher that I'd run out of petrol, couldn't wake anyone from the house and had eventually given up and walked back to the hotel. He plainly didn't believe me."

"He'd not believe the Pope," Laurie offered sympathetically. To Uncle Toby, said, "If ever Frobisher asks for a transfer to Chingford, I'll be resigning. I'm sorry, but there it is."

Uncle Toby laughed. "Don't worry, son, if that ever happens, I'll be resigning with you!"

"Anyway," Ed continued for his stepfather, "the hotel confirmed the petrol situation, and there was no trace of any finger or footprints or anything of Pa's anywhere as he had only knocked at the front door, so with no evidence the police had to believe Pa. Turns out now, of course, that Mr What's his name...?"

"Truman," Peter filled in for him.

"Yes, Truman *had* seen Pa walking home along the lane, and also confessed that he'd been sabotaging various people's show entries. Although we already knew that, but the cops have far more important things to attend to than jealous mischief-making."

"Are you implying that my cucumbers are not important!" Alf protested with a laugh.

Elsie added, "Or Captain Dowd's roses?"

Peter concluded his tale as we started on the apple crumble. "So, it seems the boy – Oleander? Not much of a name for a young lad is it? – has been charged for murder, although as he's simple-minded I suspect he'll go to some sort of institution, not prison."

"Poor Ollie," Elsie said, "Those girls never cared much for the lad. They were always blaming him for anything that went wrong, and he hasn't the wit to defend himself."

"It's partly my own fault that I was under suspicion," Peter revealed as he poured cream on his second helping of crumble. "Too many people, including Ivy, knew that I was finding Rose difficult. She was a nightmare to work with, and I knew that once I told her the TV show was to be cancelled all hell would be let loose, so I kept putting it off. I admit, her death got me out of a very tight spot."

"So Ivy is also off the hook?" I said.

"Seems so," Laurie answered. "Frobisher has put his case against Ollie, and it appears to be sticking."

"I'm not convinced," Uncle Toby said, shaking his head and frowning. "The boy's disability is too much of a convenience. And Ivy has everything to gain."

Laurie agreed with him. "But there's no way of proving anything is there?"

Uncle Toby could only nod. "Unless Ivy comes clean, no way at all."

"Perhaps he'll be better off in a proper institution?" I suggested.

Although I somehow doubted it.

POSTSCRIPT

That evening, after Peter, Ed and Puppet had gone – with firm promises to stay in touch and meet up again – Alf beckoned me into his office, wanting a quiet word.

My heart sank. He was going to tell me that he'd managed to lose my manuscript. It had taken me years to write, and it was the only copy. How I was going to start all over again from scratch I didn't know.

My apprehension increased when he sheepishly asked me to sit down in the comfortable chair. "I've a confession, Jan," he started.

Here we go, I thought.

"Your story," he went on, "I'm afraid I read some of it, and, well..."

He's going to tell me it's rubbish and he used the paper to light the fire. (Which was nonsense, because they hadn't needed a fire while I was there.)

"It was probably wrong of me, Jan, but I read some of it and I think it's really good, so I gave it to Nancy to read. As you know, she's a publisher."

I looked up at him, unable to say a word, but I could feel my heart pounding in my chest.

"She read through it yesterday, phoned me this morning. She says there's a lot of editing and polishing to do, but loves it and wants to offer you a contract for a three-book deal. If you're interested."

Honestly, as my future father-in-law I loved Alf dearly, but he could be such a chump at times. I think my squeal of excitement, and the fact that I leapt up to give him the biggest hug he'd ever experienced was quite a sufficient enough answer.

AUTHOR'S NOTE AND ACKNOWLEDGEMENTS

Thank you, as always, to Cathy Helms for the cover design and graphics, and for formatting this book. To Annie for her editing, and Connie, Elizabeth, Anna and a few of my other reader/writer friends for perusing pre-final versions for me. Any missed typos are my fault.

Thank you to Alison, the current Secretary of our Village Flower and Vegetable Show. (Yes, it is a real, annual event.) Especially, thank you for loaning me some of the old 1970s schedules to look at. It was quite fascinating to compare what was included – or not included – back then. Most notable was that the women tended to enter the 'domestic' classes, while the men favoured the gardening and growing. 2026 will be the Village Show's 100th event. I'm looking forward to it. (And hopefully winning a rosette, if not a trophy!)

Thank you, also, to the *real* Heather who has laughed with me about the portrayal of her fictional character of Chappletawton's much loved shopkeeper, postmistress – and annual show organiser. I hope she enjoys reading her fictional appearances as much as I enjoy writing them. (Especially the Hanging Baskets inclusion, which has become an actual ongoing joke between us on account of her beating my husband one year and thus receiving the coveted trophy which we had held for two years!)

A couple of mentions about some other 1970s historical context. When I started writing this series (with *A*

Mirror Murder, back during the first Covid lockdown), I didn't think the historical detail would be much of a problem. How wrong I was! Yes, I remember the 1970s when I went from being a teenager of sixteen in 1969 to my late twenties by the end of the '70s, but memory is proving to be very false in several areas. It isn't easy recalling how we managed without mobile phones, computers or the internet. Supermarkets were new in the '70s. As was colour TV. Even *Star Wars* in 1977 with its innovative SFX (special effects – now known as CGI), was new! I will never forget the experience of that opening sequence as the cinema rumbled and the underside of a massive Star Destroyer swept across the screen as if it had actually passed overhead. This was utterly breathtaking because it was an incredible opening – and nothing like it had ever been seen before.

New, too, in 1973 was Mike Oldfield's *Tubular Bells*. An album which, at the time being a unique concept was slow, initially, to catch on, but very quickly gathered momentum. As with Jan, the first time I heard it I was totally smitten, and I still adore Mike Oldfield's work these many years later. In fact, I wrote much of 'Mischief' whilst listening to *Tubular Bells I, II and III, Songs of Distant Earth,* and *TreS Lunar*. Equally, it is very firmly in my mind where I was when I first heard *Tubular Bells*. So thank you, Mr Oldfield for sharing your genius talent.

(And I must add, I saw Mike Oldfield live in concert at the Royal Albert Hall, London. An equally unforgettable experience.)

Even that stoic British Icon, Stonehenge, has changed since I was a teenager. (I'd better say, I'm now 72.) Back in the early 1970s anyone could freely go right up to the stones to inspect and touch them. But because of increasing erosion they were fenced off in 1977, and apart from special permission for the Solstices, they remain 'out of bounds'. I remember going right up to them in the snow and feeling awed by their silent presence.

Some 'detail' I have taken a liberty with. As I mentioned above, our Village Flower and Vegetable Show schedule of entry categories has changed quite a lot since the 1970s. There were sideshow events such as five-aside football, tug-of-war, tombola and 'fairground-type' entertainments. These no longer exist (apart from children's sports and a dog show), but I have taken the liberty of including a few of our modern-day flower, vegetable and crafts classes because I am familiar with them. And, well, I won a couple of them a couple of times!

Next time, Jan and Laurie will be involved in a riverside adventure with a gypsy caravan, a robin's nest inconveniently built in a postbox, and something unpleasant in a countryside fridge… *A Matter of Murder* will be the seventh Jan Christopher Cosy Mystery, and will be coming soon.

Meanwhile, if you haven't read the others in the series… might I ask why not?

Helen Hollick
Devon 2025

FURTHER PRAISE FOR HELEN HOLLICK'S NOVELS

"Helen Hollick has it all! She tells a great story, gets her history right, and writes consistently readable books" Bernard Cornwell

"A novel of enormous emotional power" Elizabeth Chadwick

"In the sexiest pirate contest, Cpt Jesamiah Acorne gives Jack Sparrow a run for his money!" Sharon K. Penman

"Thanks to Hollick's masterful storytelling Harold's nobility and heroism enthral to the point of engendering hope for a different ending to the famous battle of 1066" Publisher's Weekly

"If only all historical fiction could be this good" Historical Novel Association Reviews

"Most impressive" The Lady

"Helen Hollick's series about piratical hero Jesamiah Acorne and his mystical wife Tiola Oldstagh provides a real comfort read that seamlessly blends history, fantasy, and romance with plenty of action and suspense while also further developing the characters with every new book."

"Loved this book as I have all the previous ones. Good story, excellent characters, well written with just enough descriptive detail of shipboard life and ways."

"I completely gobbled this one up! Captain Jesamiah Acorne has become a bit of an addiction for me."

"I really love this series from Helen Hollick. As usual she is very meticulous with historical facts and as usual you won't be able to put it down."

ABOUT HELEN HOLLICK

First accepted for traditional publication in 1993, Helen became a *USA Today* Bestseller with her historical novel, *The Forever Queen* (titled *A Hollow Crown in the UK*) with the sequel, *Harold the King* (US: *I Am The Chosen King*) being novels that explore the events that led to the Battle of Hastings in 1066.

Her *Pendragon's Banner Trilogy* is a fifth-century version of the Arthurian legend, and she writes a nautical adventure/fantasy series, *The Sea Witch Voyages* alongside her *Jan Christopher Murder Mysteries*, set in the 1970s, with the first in the series, *A Mirror Murder* incorporating her, often hilarious, memories of working as a library assistant.

Her non-fiction books are *Pirates: Truth and Tale*s and *Life of A Smuggler*, and with the assistance of her daughter *Ghost Encounters: the lingering spirits of North Devon.*

She lives with her family in an eighteenth-century farmhouse in North Devon with their dogs and cats, while on the farm there are horses, Exmoor ponies, an old Welsh pony, geese, several ducks, peacocks, numerous hens and occasionally, some sheep, lambs and calves. And a few friendly, resident ghosts.

Website: www.helenhollick.net
All Helen's books are available on Amazon:
https://viewauthor.at/HelenHollick

Main Blog:
https://ofhistoryandkings.blogspot.com/
Facebook:
https://www.facebook.com/helen.hollick
X (Twitter): @HelenHollick
https://twitter.com/HelenHollick
public email: author@helenhollick.net

ALSO BY HELEN HOLLICK

THE PENDRAGON'S BANNER TRILOGY

The Kingmaking: Book One

Pendragon's Banner: Book Two

Shadow of the King: Book Three

THE SAXON 1066 SERIES

A Hollow Crown (UK edition title)

The Forever Queen (US edition title. USA Today bestseller)

Harold the King (UK edition title)

I Am The Chosen King (US edition title)

1066 Turned Upside Down

(alternative short stories by various authors)

THE SEA WITCH VOYAGES OF
CAPTAIN JESAMIAH ACORNE

Sea Witch: The first voyage

Pirate Code: The second voyage

Bring It Close: The third voyage

Ripples In The Sand: The fourth voyage

On The Account: The fifth voyage

Gallows Wake: The sixth voyage

To follow

Jamaica Gold, The seventh voyage

*

When The Mermaid Sings

A short read prequel to the Sea Witch Voyages

NON-FICTION

Pirates: Truth and Tales

Life of a Smuggler: In Fact and Fiction

Ghost Encounters: The Lingering Spirits Of North Devon

ANTHOLOGY SHORT STORIES

by various authors, including contributions by Helen Hollick

1066 Turned Upside Down (alternative stories about The Battle of Hastings)

Betrayal

Historical Stories of Exile

Fate: Tales of History, Mystery and Magic

BEFORE YOU GO

Leave a review on Amazon
https://mybook.to/MischiefOfMurder
'Like' and 'follow' where you can
Subscribe to a newsletter
Give your favourite books as presents
Spread the word!

Thank You